DON'T START ME TALKING LYRICS 1984 – 1999

PAUL KELLY

DON'T START ME TALKING LYRICS 1984 – 1999

Illustrations by Spencer P. Jones

ALLEN & UNWIN

First published in 1999 by
Allen & Unwin
9 Atchison Street
St Leonards NSW 1590
Australia
Phone: (61 2) 8425 0100
Fax: (61 2) 9906 2218
E-mail: frontdesk@allen-unwin.com.au
Web: http://www.allen-unwin.com.au

National Library of Australia
Cataloguing-in-Publication entry:

Kelly, Paul, 1955– .
Don't start me talking: lyrics 1984–1999.

Includes index.
ISBN 1 86508 105 1.

1. Rock music—Australia—1981–1990—Texts. 2. Rock
music—Australia—1991–2000—Texts. 3. Protest songs—
Australia—Texts. I. Title.

783.1421661592

Designed by Phil Campbell

Set in 10.2/13 pt Aldine by Midland Typesetters, Maryborough, Victoria
Printed by Griffin Press Pty Ltd, Adelaide

1 3 5 7 9 10 8 6 4 2

For John and Josephine

CONTENTS

All the words in this book are connected to music. Often the music is kinder to them than the page is. Music forgives them and, if it's doing its job properly, obscures the weak lines and charges the good ones. All I've ever tried to do is join the two together—something utterly simple and deeply mysterious.

Music comes first, usually stabs of phrases sung over a band jamming or melodies mumbled late at night into a small tape recorder, no proper words yet but a kind of proto-language somewhere between sounds and words (swords? wounds? swoons? the language of little deaths); and then the fall from grace, from possibility to actuality, from dream words to real words, the real words always a little disappointing at first, bald and skinny until they are sung over and over again and the dream words disappear and the real words approach sound again.

Printing the words in a book is a further stripping. Pinned on the page they no longer float in the air. Exposure brings clarity and a fresh look. Some lyrics cower, trying to hide, while others stand proud and independent as if to say, 'We don't need the music any more. We're free at last.' Being seen and not heard, not rocking on waves of sound, they can run to a different rhythm, take on a new life, show their true colours. Now they are entirely on their own.

P.K.

February 1999

I don't have what you would call a philosophy or coherent world view so I shall have to limit myself to describing how my heroes love, marry, give birth, die and speak.
ANTON CHEKHOV

POST
1985

From St Kilda To Kings Cross
Incident On South Dowling
Look So Fine, Feel So Low
White Train
Luck
Blues For Skip
Adelaide
Satisfy Your Woman
(You Can Put Your) Shoes Under My Bed
Standing On The Street Of Early Sorrows
Little Decisions

Cool Hand Lukin
Laughing Boy
Give Me One More Chance

FROM ST KILDA TO KINGS CROSS

From St Kilda to Kings Cross is thirteen hours on a bus
I pressed my face against the glass and watched the white lines
   rushing past
And all around me felt like all inside me
And my body left me and my soul went running

Have you ever seen Kings Cross when the rain is falling soft?
I came in on the evening bus, from Oxford Street I cut across
And if the rain don't fall too hard everything shines
   just like a postcard
Everything goes on just the same
Fair-weather friends are the hungriest friends
I keep my mouth well shut, I cross their open hands

I want to see the sun go down from St Kilda Esplanade
Where the beach needs reconstruction, where the palm trees
   have it hard
I'd give you all of Sydney harbour (all that land, all that water)
For that one sweet promenade

INCIDENT ON SOUTH DOWLING

My baby was dying
Turning so blue
Four feet from me dying
My head was like glue

I couldn't save my baby
(He couldn't save his baby)

Loaded and sinking
To the vegetable zone
She just kept on sinking
Now she's mineral and bone

I couldn't save my baby
(He couldn't save his baby)

We lived on the first floor
We lived in two rooms
Now my poor baby
She lives with the worms

A head full of rocks
Is a heavy, heavy head
I was watching a movie
Night of the Living Dead
Now people they whisper
Now people they stare
They say I couldn't save her
Even though I was right there

I couldn't save my baby
(He couldn't save his baby)

We lived on the first floor
We lived in two rooms
Now my poor baby
She lives with the worms

LOOK SO FINE, FEEL SO LOW

I've been seen on the street
Wearing brand new clothes
I guess I've landed on my feet
I'm lucky I suppose
She tells me that she loves me
She buys me things
She wants to take care of me
And all I gotta do is sing, sing, sing, sing
Well I look so fine
But I feel so low
Yeah I look so fine
But I feel so low

She takes me by the arm
She takes me all around
She knows all her friends are talking
Saying look what our good girl's found
One thing she's got on you
She's so easy to impress
When she asks me dumb questions
All I gotta do is say yes, yes, yes, yes
Well I look so fine
But I feel so low
Yeah I look so fine
But I feel so low

WHITE TRAIN

Standing at my doorway
I wondered why his hand was painted red
'It's just a scratch' he said
Here we go again
We stumbled to the car
By the time we hit Prince Henry's he was white
I said 'You look such a sight'
He said 'I don't feel no pain'

And I know just what to do
And I know it's nothing new
We've been through this before
And I must follow
Why must it be you (on a white train)?

I stuck until the end
Though you said I was no friend
But you were blind
I was much too kind
On a white train
Some will swill and some will sip
Some just find a place where they don't slip
Others take a kip
On a white train

And I know just what to do
And I know it's nothing new
We've been through this before
And still I follow
Why must it be you (on a white train)?

LUCK

Well it hasn't changed yet
Each time I wake in a sweat
And the sun has slipped out of the sky
As I get to my feet and struggle to dress
All my fingers are thumbs, there's a fog in my brain
Only one thing is clear—I'm late for my train
And I know all at once that it's goodbye my one
I'll be here when you're gone

Then I stumble outside
Try to flag down a ride
But the taxis just pass me by
So I run down the street, jump on a slow bus
When I get to the station the train is still there
I can't find my ticket, everybody just stares
And I'm turning to stone
As the train starts to groan
I just can't get on

I can see tomorrow
Long, black train I follow
When it's all there in your eyes
And it's all no big surprise
Well it's goodbye my one
I'll be here when you're gone
I just can't get on

Yeah it's goodbye my one
I'll be here when you're gone
I just can't get on
'Cause I'm turning to stone
As the train starts to groan
I just can't get on

BLUES FOR SKIP

Babe, there's no water in the well
Babe, there's no water in the well
I got a funny feeling we're in for quite a spell

Babe, I can't find a vein
Babe, I can't find a vein
I'm digging and I'm digging, I got the shaft again

Little cloud, little cloud way up in the air
Little cloud, little cloud way up in the air
Well I just ain't receiving, little cloud's moved on somewhere

Babe, there's no water in the well
Babe, there's no water in the well
I'm digging and I'm digging . . .

ADELAIDE

The wisteria on the back verandah is still blooming
And all the great aunts are either insane or dead
Kensington Road runs straight for a while before turning
We lived on the bend; it was there I was raised and fed
Counting and running as I go
Down past the hedges all in a row
In Adelaide, Adelaide

Dad's hands used to shake but I never knew he was dying
I was thirteen, I never dreamed he could fall
And all the great aunts were red in the eyes from crying
I rang the bells, I never felt nothing at all
All the king's horses, all the king's men
Cannot bring him back again

Find me a bar or a girl or guitar, now where do you go
   on a Saturday night?
I own this town, I spilled my wine at the bottom of the statue
   of Colonel Light
And the streets are so wide, everybody's inside
Sitting in the same chairs they were sitting in last year
(This is my town!)
All the king's horses, all the king's men
Wouldn't drag me back again
To Adelaide, Adelaide, Adelaide, Adelaide . . .

SATISFY YOUR WOMAN

Brothers let me tell you
A thing or two I know
If you don't treat your woman right
Out of the blue one day she's gonna go

When there's food upon the table
And whisky on the shelf
And good loving strong
And good loving long
She don't ever need nobody else

Satisfy your woman
So she listens for your coming
Make her feel like someone
Make her feel human
When all is said and done it's up to you

When you tell her that you love her
Make the words sound right
Tell her whenever you're thinking of her
You always got an appetite

And if you play around a little
Just make her realise
You were just testing your mettle
And that's all a different kettle
She's the sweetest fish you ever fried

Satisfy your woman
So she listens for your coming
Make her feel like someone
Make her feel human
When all is said and done it's up to you

(YOU CAN PUT YOUR) SHOES UNDER MY BED

It's a pretty pass
How you always seem to land on your feet
A little undone
Anybody else by now would be cold meat
Whenever you fall
You can put your shoes under my bed

Anytime, anytime you're passing by this way
Remember you will always have a place to stay
Whenever you call
You can put your shoes under my bed

Trip the light
And who of us can tell what's real and what's fantastic
You do it right
No one else could have such grace and be so spastic
Let heaven fall
You can put your shoes under my bed

STANDING ON THE STREET OF EARLY SORROWS

It was just a quarter mile
To your house in Kensington
It was always ninety-five degrees
(Hey Julie)

Walking to the swimming pool
February back to school
All that summer you were cool
(Hey Julie)

I'm standing on the street of early sorrows

You never know just what you've lost
Until it's yours and then it's dust
But you remain and never rust
(Hey Julie)

I'm standing on the street of early sorrows

LITTLE DECISIONS

Hard times are never over
Trouble always comes
Still I'm looking forward
To tomorrow when it comes
I've done a little damage
To myself, I didn't care
There are things a man can't manage
And that's the devil's share

Little decisions are the kind I can make
Big resolutions are so easy to break
I don't want to hear about your big decisions

Work a little harder
Keep your mind on death
Get your things in order
Take a deeper breath
If drinking is the problem
Then drink a little less
If guilt becomes a burden
Find a friend, confess

Little decisions are the kind I can make
Big resolutions are so easy to break
I don't want to hear about your big decisions

COOL HAND LUKIN

WRITTEN WITH PAUL HEWSON

I saw Dean Lukin on TV
I was drinking beer just around three
Martinez had him on the snatch
Lukin knew he had twelve and a half to catch
Ironbar from Nigeria—his leg went funny
He was out of the money

Now Cool Hand Lukin was doing some thinking
Everyone in the stadium thought he was sinking
The man called Manfred from West Germany
Fell on his back—he was history
But Cool Hand Lukin just kept coming
You can't stop Lukin when he's smoking

Well he picked it up and made a mighty sound
Then he pushed it up and held it up
Then threw it on the ground
You can't stop Lukin when he's smoking

Back in Port Lincoln they were holding their breath
Martinez and Lukin—the only ones left
At the clean and jerk he made a two-forty push
Took the gold and said 'I'm going home to fish'
And Martinez—he'd thought the medal was his
But you can't stop Lukin when he's smoking

Well he picked it up and made a mighty sound
Then he pumped it up and held it up
Then threw it on the ground
You can't stop Lukin when he's smoking

LAUGHING BOY
FOR BRENDAN BEHAN

Laughing boy is drownded
He danced on nimble toes
Angel's wit and Caesar's head
He sang The Old Dark Rose for free
Ah you should have seen him dancing on the tables!
It was just like a play
Laughing boy, laughing boy, it's over

Laughing boy is drownded
He sailed across the sea
Whiskey his daily bread
His like we'll never see again
Stay awhile, hold your hour and have another
Yeah it's just like a play!
Laughing boy, laughing boy, it's over

Dublin streets are quiet tonight
There's a shadow on the water

Well he can't stand up and he can't stay down
But he wants to get up and he wants to stay down
And he hates himself and he hates the crowd
He wants to be alone, he wants to be surrounded
Laughing boy, laughing boy, it's over

Dublin streets are quiet tonight
There's a shadow on the water

Walking on the water
Walking on the water
Walking on the water
Walking on the water

GIVE ME ONE MORE CHANCE

Give me one more chance, honey
Maybe one more chance, honey
I took you for granted
I must have been blind
I made you unhappy
I acted unkind

I apologise, honey
You've cut me down to size, honey
I know you're thinking
It's what I deserve
But now I'm pleading
It's taking some nerve
Give me one more chance

This chance I'll take it
And make it work
This promise I won't break it
Or trample it in the dirt

Listen to my cry, honey
This time I'm gonna try, honey
If I could just take back
That one last straw
You'll see I won't act like
I used to before
Give me one more chance

This chance I'll take it
I'll make it work
This promise I won't break it
'Cause I know what it's worth

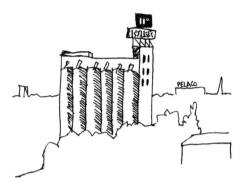

GOSSIP
1986

Last Train To Heaven
Leaps And Bounds
Before The Old Man Died
Down On My Speedway
Randwick Bells
Before Too Long
I Won't Be Torn Apart
Going About My Father's Business
Somebody's Forgetting Somebody
   (Somebody's Letting Somebody Down)
The Ballroom
Tighten Up
I've Come For Your Daughter
So Blue
The Execution
Maralinga (Rainy Land)
Darling It Hurts
Stories Of Me
Don't Harm The Messenger
Gossip
After The Show

Bradman

LAST TRAIN TO HEAVEN

This is the very last train
This is the train I'm on
This is the very last train
This is the train I'm on

People get ready
People get moving
People get rolling
People get on it

LEAPS AND BOUNDS

WRITTEN WITH CHRIS LANGMAN

I'm high on the hill
Looking over the bridge
To the MCG
And way up on high
The clock on the silo
Says eleven degrees
I remember, I remember

I'm breathing today
The month of May
All the burning leaves
I'm not hearing a sound
My feet don't even
Touch the ground
I remember, I remember
I go leaps and bounds

Down past the river
And across the playing fields
The fields all empty
Only for the burning leaves
I remember, I remember
I go leaps and bounds
I remember everything

BEFORE THE OLD MAN DIED

I used to walk in shadows
I stayed out of the sun
I used to sort information
And I used to pass it on

Before the Old Man died
Before we came alive
Before the Old Man died

I used to follow orders
Did my duty like a son
But I fell in love with whispers
And I turned them into songs

Before the Old Man died
Before we came alive
Before the Old Man died

For the way he ruined our mother
Not enough blood can run
We had plans, me and my brother
Every day I cleaned my gun

Before the Old Man died
Before we came alive
Before the Old Man Died
Before we came alive

DOWN ON MY SPEEDWAY

C'mon, Suzie, let's get ready to go
We'll be out of this town before the sun is low
I got a racetrack running in my head
The present, past and the future dead
Down on my speedway

Keep your eye on number four
They strap him inside a welded door
C'mon and tangle deep down in my wires
There's something smoking, must be fire
Down on my speedway

Mash your starter, jump your connection
This terraplane needs a fuel injection
I got a racetrack running in my head
The present, past and the future dead
Down on my speedway

RANDWICK BELLS

Randwick bells are ringing
Must be Saturday
I woke late in the middle of the day
Must be Saturday

Put a blanket on the window
And come on back to bed
We got nowhere to be and no place to go
So come on back to bed

We're gonna rise up singing
We're gonna rise up singing

Randwick bells are ringing
Through the empty rooms
The bells are ringing high and wide
For the bride and groom

Put a blanket on the window
And come on back to bed
Just for a little while
We got nowhere to be
No place to go at all, no
So come on back to bed
I'll make you smile

We're gonna rise up singing
We're gonna rise up singing
Randwick bells are ringing
Randwick bells are ringing

BEFORE TOO LONG

Before too long
The one that you're loving
Will wish that he'd never met you
Before too long
He who is nothing
Will suddenly come into view
So let the time keep rolling on
It's on my side
Lonely nights will soon be gone
High is the tide

Before too long
We'll be together
And no one will tear us apart
Before too long
The words will be spoken
I know all the action by heart
As the night-time follows day
I'm closing in
Every dog will have his day
Any dog can win

Shut the shade, do not fear anymore
Here I come creeping round your back door

Before too long
I'll be repeating
What's happened before in my mind
Before too long
Over and over
Just like a hammer inside

As the night-time follows day
I'm closing in
Every dog will have his day
Any dog can win

Before too long
Before too long

I WON'T BE TORN APART

I guess it's common knowledge
There's quite a lot of mileage
In someone else's marriage
Oh baby, I won't be torn apart

You can chuck me out now
You can lock me out now
You can break my stuff but
Baby, I won't be torn apart

From a dream I've woken
And it just can't be spoken
What remains unbroken
Oh baby, I won't be torn apart

GOING ABOUT MY FATHER'S BUSINESS

Standing in the darkness watching while you sleep
I can hear you softly breathing while I creep
Going about my father's business
Doing my father's time
What's done to me I'll do to mine

I woke up one summer morning—he was gone
Soft light through the window breaking for my son
Going about my father's business
Doing my father's time
What's done to me I'll do to mine

Know them by what they do
Let no one speak for you
Just this I beg of you
Forgive me, forgive me

Someday when we sign the treaty I'll be home
War is long and lasts forever and I'm your own
Going about my father's business
Doing my father's time
What's done to me I'll do to mine
What's done to me I'll do to mine

SOMEBODY'S FORGETTING SOMEBODY
(SOMEBODY'S LETTING SOMEBODY DOWN)

Are you lonesome tonight?
Are you feeling like me?
I'll bet you're dancing tonight
Running around so carelessly
Somebody's forgetting somebody
Somebody's letting somebody down

The door to my heart
Your kiss is the key
The keys to the car
Now they're useless to me
Somebody's forgetting somebody
Somebody's letting somebody down

And every time I hear those bells
I think I'm done for
And every time they cast their spell
I think I'm done for
Nowhere to run for
Somebody's forgetting somebody
Somebody's letting somebody down

THE BALLROOM

I went down to the Ballroom
She was dancing with her new fool
She said 'Paul, this is Henry'
Well I never know what to say when I meet 'em

I was taken to a party
I was accused of being deliberately downhearted
She said 'Paul, why so gloomy?'
Well I never know what to say when I meet 'em

Your wine tastes fine
Your friends are talking to me
I'd like to hide
Guess I'm all tongue-tied

Henry's gonna meet the family
They're gonna have him over for roast lamb next Sunday
Well good luck and I'm glad it's you
'Cause I never know what to say when I meet 'em

I was going home on Fitzroy
She was walking with her new boy
She said 'Paul, this is Tommy'
Well I never know what to say when I meet 'em

TIGHTEN UP

Mama don't like your holey shoes
Scrapping in the back yard—four be two
Daddy's smokin' motor didn't make it up the hill
Mama can't pay, she got one day
She got no money for the telephone bill
Tighten up, tighten up
Everything falls apart

Mama says to Papa now 'Where ya been?'
Papa says 'I'm sorry Mama, I got a full skin'
Mama get excited, she having an attack
Mama spins round, Daddy hits the ground
For too long now she's been taking up the slack
Tighten up, tighten up
Everything falls apart

Jimmy coming home now—see him on the run
Mama's going through the cupboards, looking for a can
Daddy on a ladder, TV on the blink
Mama can't think, Daddy's feeling like a drink
And all the dirty dishes, lord, are piling up the sink!
Tighten up, tighten up
Everything falls apart
Tighten up, tighten up
Everything falls apart

I'VE COME FOR YOUR DAUGHTER

Hello, Mr Brown
How do you slumber?
I know your street
I've got your number
Your sweet young girl
She's got the yen
Your lack of sleep
Has just begun

I've come for your daughter
I've come for your daughter
I'm crazy about that child
We drive each other wild

Believe your fears
I'm no invention
I'm on your stairs
There's no prevention

I've come for your daughter
I've come for your daughter
I'm crazy about that child
We drive each other wild

SO BLUE
FOR PAUL CEZANNE

Standing in a bright lit room
Strangers all around me
To the spot my feet were glued
Before the Lac d'Annecy
I walked around then I came back
And stood there lost in wonder
Nothing else there could attract
The rest were only pictures
So blue, so blue, so blue

I waited on a cold highway
Throwing stones and singing
A man he took me all the way
Right through to Central Station
'Where have you been?' he said to me
I've been down to the gallery
'What did you see?' he said to me
I saw the Lac d'Annecy
And it was so blue, so blue, so blue

Now colour constructs every line
And the more every link is made fine
The stronger the net will be

Every day he left his wife
To wrestle with his lover
A hundred ways Mont St Victoire
And each time starting over
Now Pablo's work was child's play
And Henri did it faster
But the slow old grizzly bear
Was their only master
So blue, so blue, so blue

THE EXECUTION

The scouts report that you've been seen down the river
They say you sleep with one eye open, one eye dreaming
Did they tell you madness passes? Did they tell you?
There's no such thing as passing madness
The monstrous has become mundane
Routine takes the place of pain
Voici le temps des assassins
You're addicted to revolution
Addiction is no revolution
Make sure your knife is sharp and clean
Make sure you're not too late, not too soon
Voici le temps des assassins
Voici le temps des assassins
Voici le temps des assassins

MARALINGA (RAINY LAND)

This is a rainy land
This is a rainy land
No thunder in our sky
No trees stretching high
But this is a rainy land

My name is Yami Lester
I hear, I talk, I touch but I am blind
My story comes from darkness
Listen to my story now unwind
This is a rainy land

First we heard two big bangs
We thought it was the Great Snake digging holes
Then we saw the big cloud
Then the big, black mist began to roll
This is a rainy land

A strangeness on our skin
A soreness in our eyes like weeping fire
A pox upon our skin
A boulder on our backs all our lives

This is a rainy land
This is a rainy land
No thunder in our sky
No trees stretching high
But this is a rainy land

My name is Edie Millipuddie
They captured me and roughly washed me down
Then my child stopped kicking

Then they took away my old man to town
They said 'Do you speak English?'
He said 'I know that Jesus loves me I know
Because the bible tells me so'

This is a rainy land
This is a rainy land
No thunder in our sky
No trees stretching high
But this is a rainy land

DARLING IT HURTS

I see you standing on the corner with your dress so high
And all the cars slow down as they go driving by
I thought you said you had some place to go
What are you doing up here putting it all on show?
Darling, it hurts to see you down Darlinghurst tonight

Do you remember, baby, how we laughed and cried?
We said we'd be together 'til the day we died
How could something so good turn so bad?
I'd do it all again because you're the best I ever had
Darling, it hurts to see you down Darlinghurst tonight

See that man with the glad hands
I want to kill him but it wouldn't be right
Now here comes another man with the glad bags
I want to break him but it's not my fight
In one hand and out the other
Baby, I don't even know why you bother
Darling, it hurts to see you down Darlinghurst tonight

STORIES OF ME

Ever since you said goodbye
I've had a reputation
I'm not drinking on the sly
I'm the star attraction
Every morning I wake up
Fill my cup and listen bitterly
To stories of me

They say a man is going round
He looks a lot like me
They say that man is going down
It's looking pretty likely
Every morning he wakes up
Fills his cup and listens shamefully
To stories of me

Everybody come on down
Set 'em up and pass 'em round
We're all here for a drowning

I was down at Baker's Hall
I heard somebody talking
That's the last thing I recall
Then my mind went walking
I woke up with a heavy head
On a hard bed trying to believe
These stories of me

Yeah I woke up in a stranger's bed
Wondering about the things she said to me
These stories of me

DON'T HARM THE MESSENGER

One day you might hear someone knocking loudly
   at your door
And you know it must be bad news—absolutely sure
You must realise before you strike the very first blow
He's the one who only tells you what you already know

Lay not a finger on him
Beat not, oh bruise not, his skinny skin skin
No don't ever harm the messenger

Understand he came a long way on a lonely road
Multiplying were his trials, heavy was his load
Understand his heart was breaking, never once did he sleep
And no hollow log kept him warm, no counsel did he keep

Give him food, give him a bed
Touch not one single hair on his head
Don't ever harm the messenger

GOSSIP

When I come home
All I want is revelation
Meat off the bone
What price is good information?
When I'm alone
I have too many companions
Chewing the phone
All I get is slender pickings
Gossip, gossip
Give us this day our daily bread
Give us this day our sweet daily bread

It makes the world go round
Over my shoulder I'm taking it down
Fish gotta swim in the sea
One thing for sure if you lie down with dogs
Then you get up with fleas

Tender no thought
Stick to the facts that invent us
This is the court
And it's called common consensus
Gossip, gossip
Give us this day our daily bread
Gossip, gossip
It makes the world go round

AFTER THE SHOW

After the show
Where shall we go?
I want to go downtown
Don't want to go uptown no more
Just want to go downtown

Wasn't it grand?
The music, the band
I know it ain't cheap
But I just can't sleep
Know what I mean

I get this feeling inside
It's just a feeling I can't hide
Oh we're gonna have some fun tonight
We're gonna ball and shout
We're gonna have a real good time
After the show

BRADMAN

Sydney, 1926, this is the story of a man
Just a kid in from the sticks, just a kid with a plan
St George took a gamble, played him in first grade
Pretty soon that young man showed them how to flash
 the blade
And at the age of nineteen he was playing for the State
From Adelaide to Brisbane the runs did not abate
He hit 'em hard, he hit 'em straight

He was more than just a batsman
He was something like a tide
He was more than just one man, he could take on any side
They always came for Bradman 'cause fortune used to hide
 in the palm of his hand

A team came out from England
Wally Hammond wore his felt hat like a chief
All through the summer of '28, '29 they gave the greencaps
 no relief
Some reputations came to grief
They say the darkest hour is right before the dawn
And in the hour of greatest slaughter the great avenger is
 being born
But who then could have seen the shape of things to come?
In Bradman's first test he went for eighteen and for one
They dropped him like a gun
Now big Maurice Tate was the trickiest of them all
And a man with a wisecracking habit
But there's one crack that won't stop ringing in his ears
'Hey Whitey, that's my rabbit'
Bradman never forgot it

He was more than just a batsman
He was something like a tide
More than just one man, he was a match for any side
Fathers took their sons 'cause fortune used to hide in the palm
of his hand

England 1930 and the seed burst into flower
All of Jackson's grace failed him, it was Bradman was
the power
He murdered them in Yorkshire, he danced for them in Kent
He laughed at them in Leicestershire; Leeds was an event
Three hundred runs he took and rewrote all the books
That really knocked those gents
The critics could not comprehend this nonchalant phenomenon
'Why this man is a machine' they said 'Even his friends say he
isn't human'
Even friends have to cut something

He was more than just a batsman
He was something like a tide
More than just one man, he was half the side
Fathers took their sons 'cause fortune used to hide in the palm
of his hand

Summer 1932 and Captain Douglas had a plan
When Larwood bowled to Bradman it was more than
man to man
And staid Adelaide nearly boiled over as rage ruled over sense
When Oldfield hit the ground they nearly jumped the fence
Now Bill Woodfull was as fine a man as ever went to wicket
And the bruises on his body that day showed that he could
stick it
But to this day he's still quoted and only he could wear it
'There are two sides out there today and only one of them's
playing cricket'

He was longer than a memory, bigger than a town
His feet they used to sparkle and he always kept them on the
    ground
Fathers took their sons who never lost the sound of the roar of
    the grandstand

Now shadows grow longer and there's so much more yet
    to be told
But we're not getting any younger, so let the part tell the whole
Now the players all wear colours, the circus is in town
I no longer can go down there, down to that sacred ground

He was more than just a batsman
He was something like a tide
More than just one man, he was half the bloody side
They always came for Bradman 'cause fortune used to hide in
    the palm of his hand

UNDER THE SUN
1987

Dumb Things
Same Old Walk
Big Heart
Don't Stand So Close To The Window
Forty Miles To Saturday Night
I Don't Remember A Thing
Know Your Friends
To Her Door
Under The Sun
Untouchable
Desdemona
Happy Slave
Crosstown
Bicentennial

Ghost Town
Already Gone
Special Treatment

DUMB THINGS

Welcome, strangers, to the show
I'm the one who should be lying low
Saw the knives out, turned my back
Heard the train coming, stayed out on the track
In the middle, in the middle, in the middle of a dream
I lost my shirt, I pawned my rings
I've done all the dumb things

Caught the fever, heard the tune
Thought I loved her, hung my heart on the moon
Started howling, made no sense
Thought my friends would rush to my defence
In the middle, in the middle, in the middle of a dream
I lost my shirt, I pawned my rings
I've done all the dumb things

And I get all your good advice
It doesn't stop me from going through these things twice
I see the knives out, I turn my back
I hear the train coming, I stay right on that track
In the middle, in the middle, in the middle of a dream
I lost my shirt, I pawned my rings
I've done all the dumb things
I melted wax to fix my wings
I've done all the dumb things
I threw my hat into the ring
I've done all the dumb things
I thought that I just had to sing
I've done all the dumb things

SAME OLD WALK

My house burned down a year ago and all your letters and
    photos I lost them
Waiting at the terminal, suddenly I see you stroll
    through customs
Your hair is long and bottle red, it used to be light brown
I nearly didn't recognise you, then my heart unwound
I see you've got the same old walk

A man is sticking close to you, you're both wearing Italian
    shoes and diamonds
And he looks so satisfied, a little on the glassy side, he's smiling
You changed the country where you live, you changed
    your second name
You changed your brand of perfume, but one thing you
    can't change
I see you've got the same old walk

The same old walk, you've even got the same old talk
Let's break the bread and pull the cork

Alex says to say hello, he would have come but he had to go
    to practice
Things are much the same around here, you know
    we've both fallen for the same actress
I'm still working on the projects, I've got my books at night
I woke up at the table, the house was burning bright
I was dreaming of the same old walk

The same old walk, you've even got the same old talk
Let's break the bread and pull the cork

My house caught fire a year ago and your books and paintings
    I lost them all

Waiting at the terminal suddenly I see you strolling through the
    customs hall
I wonder why I love you, I guess it's just because
The one who thinks he found you doesn't realise he's lost
And yes you've got the same old walk

The same old walk, you've even got the same old talk
Let's break the bread and pull the cork

BIG HEART

Listen to me before you leave
I've got something to say to you
One thing I know, I've got good eyes
I don't like what I see
Just like a V8 under the hood
Of a car made of nails and wood
Your big heart's gonna break your little body

You light the lamp, I follow you down
I stand right by your side
Out in the dark, it's bitter, it's cold
I don't much like this ride
Sometimes the motor never can stop
Sometimes the wine overrunneth the cup
Your big heart's gonna break your little body

Everyone's asleep, you're still awake
You know you give more than I can take
Your big heart's gonna break your little body

DON'T STAND SO CLOSE TO THE WINDOW

WRITTEN WITH ALEXANDER McGREGOR

Oh Marlene, how we fell
What we've done now we never can tell
Bottle of wine, then another
Suddenly we fell into each other

Don't stand so close to the window
Somebody out there might see

Then the word on the wire
Would be just like Ash Wednesday bushfire
Kiss me quick, kiss me warm
Put your dress on and hurry back home

Don't stand so close to the window
Somebody out there might see
And you're not supposed to be here with me

There's a way, there's a track
One false move and there's no turning back
Turn the page, close the book
Walk out the door now with never a look

And don't stand so close to the window
Somebody out there might see
And you're not supposed to be here with me
The walls have ears and the darkness has eyes don't you see?

FORTY MILES TO SATURDAY NIGHT

Well I rubbed the dirt all down
And I washed away six aching days
And my shoes all slick and spit
And my singlet fresh and my sideburns shaved
As I turn from the mirror
And I open my first beer since yesterday

Danny brings the Bedford round
A three-ton girl with a ten-foot tray
And she knows the way to town
So we kiss goodbye to two weeks pay
Now the leaves are shaking
And the stars are all waking from the day

Big wheel turning (turning all night)
Big light burning (burning so bright)
Downright foolish but that's alright
It's only forty miles to Saturday night!

There's a place on Fortune Street
And a band down there called Gunga Din
And Joanne from Miner's Creek
She said that she'd be back again
She lives out on the station
And she works on my imagination

Big wheel turning (turning all night)
Big light burning (burning so bright)
Downright foolish but that's alright
It's only forty miles to Saturday night!

I DON'T REMEMBER A THING

I woke up one morning, my head was feeling sore
Woke up to the sound of knocking, detectives at my door
There were two of them, they walked right in, I said 'What's
     going on?'
The sergeant shook his head and said 'Don't you know what
     you have done?'
I don't remember a thing

They took me to a house, I knew that I'd been there before
There were men with tape and pencils, there was blood upon
     the floor
The sergeant asked me softly 'Now do you recall?'
It all looked so familiar as though I'd dreamt it all
I don't remember a thing

There was a photo on the dresser of a man who looked like me
He was kissing a girl all in white, she was sitting on his knee
A note was on the mantle, written in my hand
It said 'I love you, darling, more than I can stand'
I don't remember a thing

KNOW YOUR FRIENDS

She catches taxis, he likes walking to the station
She goes to parties, he goes with her just to please her
They go round—round and round
Out at a restaurant she's a little high and mighty
He wants to kiss her, he's full of piss and peace and beauty
They go round—round and round
Know your friends, know your friends
You gotta have one, one to lean on
She has a problem with some man who stayed and then ran
He's understanding but oh how his heart is breaking
They go round—round and round
Know your friends, know your friends
You gotta have one, one to lean on

TO HER DOOR

They got married early, never had much money
Then when he got laid off they really hit the skids
He started up his drinking, then they started fighting
He took it pretty badly, she took both the kids
She said 'I'm not standing by to watch you slowly die
So watch me walking out the door'
She said 'Shove it, Jack, I'm walking out the fucking door'

She went to her brother's, got a little bar work
He went to the Buttery, stayed about a year
Then he wrote a letter, said I want to see you
She thought he sounded better so she sent him up the fare
He was riding through the cane in the pouring rain
On Olympic to her door

He came in on a Sunday, every muscle aching
Walking in slow motion like he'd just been hit
Did they have a future? Would he know his children?
Could he make a picture and get them all to fit?
He was shaking in his seat, riding through the streets
In a Silvertop to her door

UNDER THE SUN

I went out one morning, I stood on the shoreline again
Maybe I was dreaming as the light came streaming in
Memory and rhyme bringing back the time
Everything under the sun

Leaving South Fremantle in a Falcon panel van
We were smoking Marlboro, always singing Barbara Ann
Spinning out our dreams, making up our schemes
All day long under the sun

I can see them all so clearly now they're gone
They're flying, they're dying one by one

We were microscopic, swarming in the honey sun
We thought we were endless, couldn't see
    our friendship undone
Colourful and strange, a kind of life endangered
On the turn under the sun

UNTOUCHABLE

She breaks in on a dollar everywhere she goes
She leads him on more than she will ever know
Untouchable and it's such a crime
I find her ways are always taking up my mind
Untouchable—I'm the one to fall
Untouchable—and I come each time she calls
She breaks in on a friendship everywhere she goes
I find her ways are always taking up my mind
Get down on my knees just for her
Tell the world I do adore her
Untouchable just like water flows
Untouchable when she's taking off her clothes
She breaks in on a dollar everywhere she goes
I find her ways are always taking up my mind

DESDEMONA

Once I had a life so rare
Beauty lived inside the lair
Desdemona straight and true
Desdemona gold and blue
Well I lost my Desdemona
With my own hands I destroyed her
Yes I lost my Desdemona
I fell for lies, I fell for lies

Poison in my ear at night
Took away my appetite
I couldn't hold on to the pain
Something broke inside my brain
Well I lost my Desdemona
With my own hands I destroyed her
Yes I lost my Desdemona
I fell for lies, I fell for lies

Never has a man been born
Who can take a woman's scorn
Nor tasted a more bitter wine
Than the brewing of his mind
Yes I lost my Desdemona
With my own hands I destroyed her
Yes I lost my Desdemona
I fell for lies, I fell for lies

HAPPY SLAVE

A tug comes on the wire, duty calls me now
She says 'My land is useless and I need some kind of plough'
(She's my kind of driver)
I'm upstanding straight away, I'm ready for my toil
I feel her whip cracking on my back as I dig into her soil
(She's my kind of driver)

I'm burning up her cane, I'm threshing in her barn
She keeps me at my business until I'm breaking down
I'm working way too hard, I never get to save
But I don't mind, I don't mind, I'm a happy slave

And when my work is done I'm ready to explode
Suddenly I'm flying when she takes my heavy load
(She's my kind of driver)

I'm tending to her flock, I'm burning up her cane
I never can refuse her and I never complain
I'm working way too hard, I never get to save
But I don't mind, I don't mind, I'm a happy slave

CROSSTOWN

Crosstown, under the freeway, late at night
Crosstown, over the river shining bright
I reach my destination and I find her arms waiting to hold me
Her love is mine

She lives high on the hillside, ain't no shack
She's got anything she wants, she don't lack
Daddy calls her his precious but he would die
If he knew what his darling daughter did on the sly

And when we can't be together I call my imagination
Takes me over the water
Crosstown is around the world

Now I'm working the night shift every night
And I'm doing the day shift none too bright
But I'm keeping my head down, doing time
'Cause I'm working to make her, working to make her mine

And when we can't be together I call my imagination
Takes me over the water
Crosstown is around the world

BICENTENNIAL

A ship is sailing into harbour
A party's waiting on the shore
And they're running up the flag now
And they want us all to cheer

Charlie's head nearly reaches the ceiling
But his feet don't touch the floor
From a prison issue blanket his body's swinging
He won't dance any more

Take me away from your dance floor
Leave me out of your parade
I have not the heart for dancing
For dancing on his grave

Hunted man out on the Barcoo
Broken man on Moreton Bay
Hunted man across Van Diemen's
Hunted man all swept away

Take me away from your dance floor
Leave me out of your parade
I have not the heart for dancing
For dancing on his grave

GHOST TOWN

Today I thought I saw you
Standing on the corner
I was just about to call your name, I nearly touched her
Then she turned and suddenly it all came crashing down
Just my imagination playing tricks in ghost town

This morning I lay sleeping
I heard soft footsteps creeping
Standing right beside me at my bed I felt your breathing
You said 'Daddy can I come inside? It's cold down in
    the ground'
The sun came in, I woke up hard and empty in ghost town

Now I wander everywhere
Talking to the air
And every day just like the day before in countless numbers
And every night the curtain falls upon the day gone down
And every single town that I pass through is a ghost town

ALREADY GONE

The moon is in the tree
The moon is in the tree
And my shit turns to water
And my shit turns to water
I get the taste of ash
I get the taste of ash
Each time we kiss
Each time we kiss
And I'm already gone
I'm already gone

A desert in my head
A desert in my head
Each time we touch
Each time we touch
I get the feel of dust
I get the feel of dust
Cover me by degrees
Cover me by degrees
And I'm already gone
I'm already gone

SPECIAL TREATMENT

Grandfather walked this land in chains
A land he called his own
He was given another name
And taken into town

He got special treatment
Special treatment
Very special treatment

My father worked a twelve-hour day
As a stockman on the station
The very same work but not the same pay
As his white companions

He got special treatment
Special treatment
Very special treatment

Mother and father loved each other well
But together they could not stay
They were split up against their will
Until their dying day

They got special treatment
Special treatment
Very special treatment

Mama gave birth to a stranger's child
A child she called her own
Strangers came and took away that child
To a stranger's home

She got special treatment
Special treatment
Very special treatment

I never spoke my mother's tongue
I never knew my name
I never learnt the songs she sung
I was raised in shame

I got special treatment
Special treatment
Very special treatment
We got special treatment
Special treatment
Very special treatment

SO MUCH WATER SO CLOSE TO HOME
1989

You Can't Take It With You
Sweet Guy
Most Wanted Man In The World
I Had Forgotten You
Stupid Song
South Of Germany
Careless
Moon In The Bed
No You
Everything's Turning To White
Pigeon/Jundamurra
Cities Of Texas

Hard Love
Beggar On The Street of Love
Hidden Things
Don't Say I'm No Good
Just A Phrase He's Going Through
Too Many Movies

I Had Too Much Loving Last Night
Pouring Petrol On A Burning Man
Other People's Houses

YOU CAN'T TAKE IT WITH YOU

You might have a happy family, nice house, fine car
You might be successful in real estate
You could even be a football star
You might have a prime time TV show seen in every home
    and bar
But you can't take it with you

You might own a great big factory, oil wells on sacred land
You might be in line for promotion, with a foolproof
    retirement plan
You might have your money in copper, textiles or imports
    from Japan
But you can't take it with you

You can't take it with you though you might pile it up high
It's so much easier for a camel to pass through a needle's eye

You might have a body of fine proportion and a hungry mind
A handsome face and a flashing wit, lips that kiss and eyes
    that shine
There might be a queue all around the block
Long before your starting time
But you can't take it with you

You might have a great reputation so carefully made
And a set of high ideals, polished up and so well displayed
You might have a burning love inside, so refined,
    such a special grade
But you can't take it with you

SWEET GUY

In the morning we wreck the bed
You bring me coffee black and boiling
Then we start up again and the coffee goes cold
I wake up drinking from your lips
Kisses warm and tender
And I'd give up the world just to see you smile

One thing I will never understand
(It's become my problem)
And it's something that's right out of my hands
(My hands are clean)
What makes such a sweet guy turn so mean?

I went to town with a moody man
A handsome Dr Jekyll
He was right by my side turning into Mr Hyde
I ran for cover but I ran too slow
I was stitched by strangers
And they shook their heads that someone could do the things
    you did

One thing I will never understand
(It's become my problem)
And it's something that's right out of my hands
(My hands are clean)
What makes such a sweet guy turn so mean?

I must be mad, I must be crazy
Everyone tells me so
Every day I see it coming
Now I'm facing the wall, waiting for the blow

In the morning you kiss my head
You say it was another
Now you're down on your knees
Begging me to forgive you please
I wake up aching from your touch
Every muscle tender
Then I look in your eyes, the way you smile
And I'm hypnotised

One thing I will never understand
(It's become my problem)
And it's something that's right out of my hands
(My hands are clean)
What makes such a sweet guy turn so mean?

MOST WANTED MAN IN THE WORLD

I'm not good looking, well built or tall
I'm not a movie star up on somebody's wall
But when I lie next to my girl
I'm the most wanted man in the world

When she calls my name in a voice soft and low
Then she calls it again, something inside of me goes
When she starts moving her hand
I'm the most wanted man in the land
I'm the most wanted man in the world

Arrest me now, take me I'm yours! I'm guilty of loving you
Hold me down, I won't fight it, I surrender!

And when I'm working miles from home
I spend all my money on the long distance telephone
When she says 'I wish you were here'
I'm the most wanted man anywhere
I'm the most wanted man in the world

I HAD FORGOTTEN YOU

I had forgotten the dress you wore
The first time I ever saw you walking through a door
And I had forgotten your secret smile
That seemed to say it's okay, you can stay awhile
And I never kept a trace
Of your voice, your touch, your taste,
Or your perfume
I had forgotten you

Then I got a letter, it came today
From an old friend; this is what he had to say
You know Frank Hannon, well, his wife just died
But the big news is he's already found another bride
You may remember her
She says you once went out with her
She was twenty-two
She still remembers you

She's been a widow for six years
Now her children have left home
She nursed Frank's wife for a while
But nobody knew this was going on

Now Mary comes to me, she turns out the light
Then after a while she asks me if I'm alright
Well I turn to hold her but I'm not there
Tonight I feel like both of us are made of air
Mary's hair is turning grey
And she worries about her weight
Do you, too?
I had forgotten you
Yes, it's true I had forgotten you
Nothing new
I had forgotten you

STUPID SONG

She's a melody; when she goes by she disturbs my soul
She's a melody and she's playing me with cool control
I try to keep a quiet heart but all in vain
I'm falling, falling in a trance again

She's a stupid song that once it's heard never goes away
She's a stupid song, sorely nagging me night and day
And just when I think she's gone, well! here she comes again
She's running around my brain

I will carve her name upon the air, not in wood or stone
I will carve her name and tell the world the beauty I've known
And when we both are dead and gone
The melody will carry on, yes, only the notes remain

SOUTH OF GERMANY

Many lives I could have lived, many trails taken
It always seems that way at twenty-three
You walk into a room sometime and then a window opens
My life changed forever in the south of Germany

A morning train I had to catch, I just lay there sleeping
There was nothing in that town to hold me
By the time the clock had done another day of creeping
My life had changed forever in the south of Germany

Oh I'm so sorry that today I have to go away

Seven children have I raised, I love some more than others
The hardest thing to do is set them free
So I learned my lesson hard seven times all over
My life changed forever in the south of Germany

I never was the kind of girl for acting sentimental
I never called our meeting destiny
I just call it good luck to meet a man so gentle
My life changed forever in the south of Germany

Oh I'm so sorry that today I have to go away

Sometimes when I wake at night I'm dreaming of another
Then I turn and touch him next to me
And I know where I belong; still I sometimes wonder
My life changed forever in the south of Germany

Oh I'm so sorry that today I have to go away

CARELESS

How many cabs in New York City, how many angels on a pin?
How many notes in a saxophone, how many tears in a
    bottle of gin?
How many times did you call my name, knock at the door
    but you couldn't get in?

I know I've been careless

I've been wrapped up in a shell, nothing could get through to me
Acted like I didn't know I had friends and family
I saw worry in their eyes, it didn't look like fear to me

I know I've been careless
I lost my tenderness
I've been careless
I took bad care of this

Like a mixture in a bottle, like a frozen over lake
Like a longtime, painted smile I got so hard I had to crack
You were there, you held the line, you're the one that brought
    me back

I know I've been careless
I lost my tenderness
I've been careless
I took bad care of this

How many cabs in New York City, how many angels on a pin?
How many notes in a saxophone, how many tears in a
    bottle of gin?
How many times did you call my name, knock at the door
    but you couldn't get in?
How many stars in the milky way, how many ways can you
    lose a friend?

MOON IN THE BED

I have the moon in my bed
Every night down she falls
I have the moon in my bed
I had nothing, now I have it all
And I have the sun in my heart
When I rise by her side
I have the sun in my heart
Even through the darkest night
She can save me from myself
Make me feel like someone else
She can take me somewhere else
Where I hardly know myself
I have the moon in my bed
I have the sun in my heart
I have the stars at my feet
I have the moon in my bed

NO YOU

I woke up with all my clothes on
Cigarette smoke in my hair
Unglued my eyes and saw a dirty room
Spilling ashtray by my bed
Empty bottle on the chair
No one else was there

I was ready in two minutes flat
Just washed my face and combed my hair
I had an eight-twenty-five train to catch
I was out of there
Flying through the front door
Then I hit the air!
No you! No you! No you! No you!
No you, no you, no you!

I was sucked into the subway
Like an ant into a hole
I stood in the crowded carriage
Shoulder to shoulder
The wheels began to roll
A tattoo in my soul

I do not lack good companions
They pick me up when I'm feeling down
We go to the track on Saturdays
Spread our money round
I go up and down
And every single sound says
No you! No you! No you! No you!
No you, no you, no you!

EVERYTHING'S TURNING TO WHITE

Late on a Friday my husband went up to the mountains
    with three friends
They took provisions and bottles of bourbon to last them
    all through the weekend
One hundred miles they drove just to fish in a stream
And there's so much water so close to home

When they arrived it was cold and dark; they set up
    their camp quickly
Warmed up with whiskey they walked to the river
    where the water flowed past darkly
In the moonlight they saw the body of a girl floating face down
And there's so much water so close to home

When he holds me now I'm pretending
I feel like I'm frozen inside
And behind my eyes, my daily disguise
Everything's turning to white

It was too hard to tell how long she'd been dead, the river was
    that close to freezing
But one thing for sure, the girl hadn't died very well to judge
    from the bruising
They stood there above her all thinking the same thoughts
    at the same time
There's so much water so close to home

They carried her downstream from their fishing
Between two rocks they gently wedged her
After all, they'd come so far, it was late
And the girl would keep, she was going nowhere
They stayed up there fishing for two days
They reported it on Sunday when they came back down
There's so much water so close to home

When he holds me now I'm pretending
Nothing is working inside
And behind my eyes, my daily disguise
Everything's turning to white

The newspapers said that the girl had been strangled to death
    and also molested
On the day of the funeral the radio reported that a young man
    had been arrested
I went to the service a stranger, I drove past the lake
    out of town
There's so much water so close to home

When he holds me now I'm pretending
Nothing is working inside
And behind my eyes, my daily disguise
Everything's turning to white

PIGEON/JUNDAMURRA

My name is Officer O'Malley
My job is hunting Pigeon down
I don't like this kind of work much
I'm sick of sleeping on the ground
Pigeon—that's the name we gave him
Pigeon used to be so tame
'Til one day he turned against his master
Killed him, broke his brother's chains

Now Pigeon could track the Holy Spirit
But he don't leave no tracks at all
I've been running round in circles
I've been feeling like a fool
Pigeon—that's the name we gave him
But he's got another name
It's spreading all across the valleys
Jundamurra!—like a burning flame

One time we had him in a gully
One time we had him in a cave
Each time we closed in on our quarry
He disappeared like smoke into a haze
Pigeon—that's the name we gave him
Pigeon—putting me to shame
I do this job because I have to
I don't say that he's to blame
Jundamurra!—how I hate that name

CITIES OF TEXAS

I am the wind without a name
I have been blowing long before you came
I am the wind no one calls
I see your towers rise and fall
Cities of Texas, my lovely ones
Cities of Texas, shining in the sun

I am the wind no one knows
Out from your deserts, down from your melting snows
Over the ocean right across your land
I turn your high glass back to shifting sand
Cities of Texas, my lovely ones
Cities of Texas, shining in the sun

HARD LOVE

I don't want a love
Changing like the wind
You know I want the kind of loving
That'll stay by me through thick and thin
I want a hard love this time
A hard love seems so hard to find

And I don't want a love
Shifting like the sand
You know I want the kind of loving
That's gonna stick, that's gonna stand
I want a hard love this time
A hard love seems so hard to find

Maybe you haven't heard
Listen up, I'm giving you the hard word
Baby don't let me down
Baby just stick around
Oooh this fire might burn your house down to the ground!

I don't want a love
Melting like the snow
You know I want the kind of loving
That's always there, doesn't come and go
I want a hard love this time
A hard love seems so hard to find

BEGGAR ON THE STREET OF LOVE

In my time I have been a rich man giving favours
All the world at my feet and its many different flavours
I sucked it all dry
Now I realise
I'm a beggar on the street of love

All the rest have no charm
There's nothing they can give me
What I want makes me poor
In this great big world of plenty
I'm holding out my cup
Only you can fill it up
I'm a beggar on the street of love

On my own I'm standing, so patiently
And my heart keeps calling, calling out for you to see
You look right through me and you pass me by

Take my hand, lead me to your loving milk and honey
Cover me, keep me from the night so cold and rainy
Please, I'm down on my knees
I'm a beggar on the street of love

HIDDEN THINGS

I don't need a man to flatter me with praises
And I don't need to wear big diamond rings
All I ever want is someone true to hold me
And surely to reveal sweet hidden things

All around this world I have been a constant traveller
I have been with presidents and kings
I have sat on steps with men who have delivered
And I have come to know some hidden things

I don't need to live in a mansion on a hillside
And watch the coloured birds as they sing
All I ever want is a love that keeps on turning
And someone who can show me hidden things

So if you find someone who says he loves you truly
Make sure that you take a look within
For a handsome face can fade and passion soon grows colder
And all that will remain are hidden things

DON'T SAY I'M NO GOOD

As I write this letter now my heart is in my hands
Maybe if I write things down we both might understand
In my imagination I can see your rage
Sitting at the kitchen table screwing up the page

But don't say I'm no good
I'm just doing what you said I should

If you take a look back at the way we've come to be
One of us was getting stronger and it wasn't me
You're the one that always said that I need you too much
You're the one that told me I should live without your crutch

So don't say I'm no good
I'm just doing what you said I should

There's a veil before your eyes
But time is on my side
One day you'll realise your foolish pride

As I end this letter now the night is coming down
All the boats are loaded softly sleeping on the sound
You know what you need isn't always what you want
You can write to me Port Lincoln poste restante

And don't say I'm no good
I'm just doing what you said I should

JUST A PHRASE HE'S GOING THROUGH

So you've found him this time
You're running all over town
Telling the world all about it
Spreading the word all around
How he loves you
And he's always thinking of you
I'm sorry to bring you bad news
It's just a phrase he's going through

It's an old situation
I've been down that same road before
And I fell for the same lines
I wanted to hear more and more
How he loved me
How he'd die for me
I'm sorry to give you the news
It's just a phrase he's going through

And it makes me feel so torn
To see you drinking all his lies dusk to dawn
And it makes me want to shake you and tell you
   that's no way to act
All that I'm saying is fact

Go ahead, foolish baby
Nothing's going to change your mind
Fly straight to the flame, child
Me I'll just follow behind
Yes he loves you
Yes he'd die for you
It's really nothing new
It's just a phrase he's going through

TOO MANY MOVIES

When I was a younger girl
I lived in a dream
Acting out all different lives
I saw on the screen
Mama said 'Now don't believe everything you see
They're just stories, not the way life is going to be
You see too many movies, too many movies
That's all the matter with you'

Now I am an older girl
I still don't know myself
Every day I try so hard
To be somebody else
And my daddy says to me 'Girl what's wrong with you'
I just say 'Well I don't want to live the way you do
'Cause I've seen too many movies, too many movies
That's all the matter with me'

Now you walk into the room
Moving kind of slow
Speaking from the corner of your mouth
And keeping low
And you try your lines on me
I gotta admire your style
But I know where you got your walk
And where you got that smile
You've seen too many movies, too many movies
That's all the matter with you
Yeah, we've seen too many movies
Too many movies
That's all the matter with me
That's all the matter with you

I HAD TOO MUCH LOVING LAST NIGHT

Got to work at the usual time
A little out of breath and my hair was flying
I rode in the elevator sixteen floors
Crowded and surrounded by the usual bores
My eyes were red and my circles were black
I could hear them buzzing all around my back
I didn't mind I was buzzing inside
I had too much loving last night

Work piled up like digging a grave
The morning went by in a kind of haze
I stopped for a coffee around half past ten
And I didn't look up 'til a quarter to one
I couldn't stop thinking about the fun we'd had
I felt so good and I felt so bad
Lunchtime came, I couldn't eat a bite
I had too much loving last night

First he teased me
Then he squeezed me
How he pleased me!
I had too much loving last night

Round four o'clock I was starting to fade
My boss looked like the Marquis de Sade
I thought about It for the ninety-ninth time
That got me through 'til closing time
Now I'm riding on the evening train
Feels like my body is one big brain
Hair still messed, I ain't talking right
I had too much loving last night

POURING PETROL ON A BURNING MAN

I've been pumping on the jack
All my lonely days are stacked
Now I'm heading straight for you
I've been working on the wire
I've been putting out these fires
Now I'm heading straight for you

Oh my angel
I'm carrying the can
Oh my angel
You're pouring petrol on a burning man

I've been changing dirty oil
Now my rags are really soiled
And I'm heading straight for you
I've been laying it too thick
I've been cleaning up the slick
Now I'm heading straight for you

Oh my angel
I'm carrying the can
Oh my angel
You're pouring petrol on a burning man

Every night above my bed
Every night inside my head
I'm heading straight for you

Oh my angel
I'm carrying the can
Oh my angel
You're pouring petrol on a burning man

His mother always let him stay up late on Fridays. They would lie in her room together watching TV. Sometimes she fell asleep before he did and he'd be watching a talk show—one person talking, then another, then all this laughter coming from nowhere. Next thing he knew she would be shaking him gently. 'Wake up little one, wake up.' Saturday morning. So he'd get up, dress himself, put his shoes on and leave the house without breakfast. Breakfast always came later in other people's houses.

They had to catch two buses to reach their destination and the trip seemed to take forever unless he fell asleep along the way. When they got off at their stop they were in a bigger, brighter neighbourhood. The houses were a long way back from the street and some of them were hidden from view by big hedges. Looking down the street was like looking through the wrong end of a telescope. His mother guided him through this country. She knew exactly where to go. She carried in her bag a big, heavy ring full of keys—all keys to other people's houses.

She would turn one of the keys in the lock. Some of the doors needed two keys. Then presto they were in. The houses had so many things in them yet still so much space. He liked to rub his feet quickly on the thick pile then touch a door knob with one finger and give himself a small electric shock. In the first house they always went straight to the refrigerator. There were things in there he couldn't imagine anyone ever eating—strange looking pastes in jars and horrible concoctions in plastic. His mother would sit him down with a jam sandwich and a glass of milk, then set to work cleaning other people's houses.

And so they would go all day long from one house to another, his mother scrubbing, mopping, vacuuming, cleaning, tidying up, leaving him to his own devices. Often, if no one was home, she would play music on the stereo. There was one record she always put on and sang along to. It had two men and two women on the cover and they all looked sort of blonde except one of the women had dark hair. The stereo flickered like the controls of a spaceship. Other houses were full of books and sometimes he was allowed to take one of the books down from the shelves and open it up. There were books on war and cricket and movie stars. He liked to look at the pictures and pick out big words that he knew. He was very careful with the books. He was very careful with everything in other people's houses.

Many of the houses had other children in them. They would rush right past him into the yard. He'd follow them out back where the backyard was as big as the house, sometimes even bigger. He'd play with them for a while then sit on the steps watching them. He felt slower than the others. There was a girl about his age who lived in a house they went to every second Saturday. Her name was Stephanie. She used to take him everywhere with her, wherever she went, all around the house, even into her room. He'd never see his mother until it was time to leave. One Saturday his mother told him that Stephanie and her family had moved away. Just like that. He still thinks of her now, twenty years later, moving, laughing, sitting down to dinner, making conversation, making love in other people's houses.

COMEDY
1990

Don't Start Me Talking
Winter Coat
It's All Downhill From Here
Brighter
Your Little Sister (Is A Big Girl Now)
I Won't Be Your Dog Anymore
Take Your Time
Sydney From A 727
I Can't Believe We Were Married
From Little Things Big Things Grow
Blue Stranger
Keep It To Yourself
Invisible Me
Little Boy Don't Lose Your Balls

Brand New Ways
Treaty
When I First Met Your Ma
Rally Round The Drum
Don't Explain
Taught By Experts

Foggy Highway
Nobody She Knows
Teach Me Tonight
Play Me
Between Two Shores
Thanks I'll Think It Over

DON'T START ME TALKING

Don't start me talking or I'll tell everything I know
Don't start me talking, I'll spill the beans for sure
Right before your eyes
I'll blow it all open wide
Don't start me talking

Don't start me talking 'cause once I get the itch
Don't start me talking, I just have to scratch
First a little slow
Then I start to flow
Don't start me talking

Cheers, all you, cheers
Help me if I fall
Cheers, all you, cheers
God bless you all

Don't start me talking or I'll have it all my way
Don't start me talking 'cause night will turn to day
Stars will run and hide
Strong men weep a tide
So don't start me talking

Cheers, all you, cheers
Help me find a wall
Cheers, all you, cheers
God bless you all

WINTER COAT

We were lovers once long ago
Walking through cold city streets like lovers do
Stopped inside a market
Kissed beside a stall
Someone said 'You'd better move on if you're not buying at all'

Then I saw the winter coat hanging on the rack
I thought about that winter coat hanging on my back
So you helped me try it on
It was just my size
Then you bought that coat for me after haggling over the price

Now when it's chilly
Up in these cold, cold hills
I just put on my winter coat
My winter coat keeps me warm

Years have come along
Years have gone
Some friends have risen
Some have moved on
And my old winter coat still hangs by my front door
Holding all the stories I don't remember anymore

And when it gets freezing
Up in these cold, cold hills
I just put on my winter coat
My winter coat keeps me warm

IT'S ALL DOWNHILL FROM HERE

I was born in a crowded taxi
Daddy scooped me right up off the floor
And he carried me up the path through the big, swinging doors

I was taught not to speak to strangers
But strangers always seemed to know my name
And they bought and sold my pleasure, my disgust
   and my shame

Now I've got debts to pay
I've got scores to settle
Dreams at break of day
Long nights in the saddle
It's all downhill from here

Every day brings changes in the mirror
Every hand that touches me is kind
When I think of home it sparkles and so brightly shines

But I've got debts to pay
I've got scores to settle
Dreams at break of day
Long nights in the saddle
It's all downhill from here

BRIGHTER

Where is your husband?
I've seen him digging snow
Blowing on his blue hands
With yards and yards to go

You're wild, you're wild, you're wild
He's just a child

It's getting brighter all the time
It's getting brighter all the time

Where is your lover boy?
I heard him on the radio
Singing a lover's story
Then the music turned to snow

You're wild, you're wild, you're wild
He's just a child

It's getting brighter all the time
It's getting brighter all the time

Here comes your law man
He's coming through fields of snow
With his pistol in his pants
And only yards to go

You're wild, you're wild, you're wild
He ain't no child

It's getting brighter all the time
It's getting brighter all the time

YOUR LITTLE SISTER (IS A BIG GIRL NOW)

She was always bugging us
Every day on the way home
Riding on the back of the bus
Every time we tried to kiss
She was there right beside us
Putting on a funny face
Your little sister's a big girl now

It seemed to happen in a dream
Like the corn at summer's end
She was standing fully grown
Peaches hanging on the tree
I shook some loose, she bit too quick
All the juice came running down
Your little sister's a big girl now

We were married in the spring
Little sister carried fresh flowers
My best friend held the ring
Later on that evening
I saw them dancing in a corner
She was kissing him slow and long
Your little sister's a big girl now
Your little sister's a big girl now
Such a big girl now

I WON'T BE YOUR DOG ANYMORE

I've been drinking muddy water
And it tastes like turpentine
I've been leaving muddy footprints
Up and down the Morgan line
Crows are crying all around me
In a sky where the sun refuse to shine

I've been taking scraps from back doors
I've been hiding in the cane
I've been fighting over morsels
And I've been slinking back again
I've been building up a reputation
On the levee, all across the plain

No I won't be your dog
Your low riding dog anymore

Now the mangrove sun is sinking
And the moon is bloody red
Every gun is clean and loaded
Lying by a feather bed
Far and wide goes my description
And the price is rising on my head

No I won't be your dog
Your low riding dog anymore

I've been drinking muddy water
I've been keeping way down low
All I hear is my own breathing
All I see is a distant glow
All I have is tearing me up
Wearing me down, just won't let me go

No I won't be your dog
Your low riding dog anymore
No I won't be your dog
Your skinny little dog anymore

TAKE YOUR TIME

This thing needs some working on
You just can't push it through
Put a little mind on the matter
I'm counting on you
Take your time

Mama gets sore with the child
Who just wants to eat and then run
She says 'Baby what's your hurry
To get this over and done?'
Take your time
Take your time
Take your time
And show me you love me

There go the bells at midnight
Ringing all out of tune
Here comes the moon arising
Sneaking into our room
So take your time
Take your time
Take your time
And show me you love me

SYDNEY FROM A 727

Have you ever seen Sydney from a 727 at night?
Sydney shines such a beautiful light
And I can see Bondi through my window way off to the right
And the curling waves on a distant break
And the sleeping city just about to wake
Have you ever seen Sydney from a 727 at night?

Now the red roofs are catching the first rays of
    the morning sun
My eyes are full of sand from my midnight run
And the captain says 'Belt up now, we'll be touching
    down in ten'
So I press my seat and I straighten up
I fold my tray and I stash my cup
As the red roofs are catching the first rays of the morning sun

Have you ever fallen for a girl with different coloured eyes?
And sent her letters full of lies
Have you ever longed to see the sun fall where it used to rise?
And quit your job on the spot
Bought that ticket, yeah, spent the lot
Have you ever fallen for a girl with different coloured eyes?

Have you ever seen Sydney from a 727 at night?
Have you ever seen Sydney from a 727 at night?
Have you ever seen Sydney from a 727 at night?
Me I've never seen Dallas from a DC9

I CAN'T BELIEVE WE WERE MARRIED

We danced in the kitchen on Boxing Day
I held you swaying in my arms to Marvin Gaye
Our Christmas ham turned green by New Year's Eve
We weren't hungry anyway
Now sometimes we see each other on the street
Maybe at a hotel or some party
We say hello, then we have to go
I can't believe we were married
That we were wed

Our houses were a shambles, our love conspiracy
Your hand was always down my pants before our guests
    could leave
They didn't like our drugs, our children or our dogs
The way we made it up each day
Now the kids have grown we talk on the phone
If one of them is sick or needs some money
Our words are dry, so measured and polite
I can't believe we were married
That we were wed

Now maybe if I'm with someone you come into my mind
The one I knew with your certain little cries
You're not the only one to come rushing in
It's like a party line

Yeah sometimes we see each other on the street
Maybe at a concert or some party
We say hello, talk about the show
I can't believe we were married
Yeah we say hello, then we have to go
You send your regards to all my family
And the years have changed even the sound of your name
I can't believe we were married
That we were wed

FROM LITTLE THINGS BIG THINGS GROW

WRITTEN WITH KEV CARMODY

Gather round people, I'll tell you a story
An eight year long story of power and pride
British Lord Vestey and Vincent Lingiarri
Were opposite men on opposite sides

Vestey was fat with money and muscle
Beef was his business, broad was his door
Vincent was lean and spoke very little
He had no bank balance, hard dirt was his floor

From little things big things grow
From little things big things grow

Gurindji were working for nothing but rations
Where once they had gathered the wealth of the land
Daily the pressure got tighter and tighter
Gurindji decided they must make a stand

They picked up their swags and started off walking
At Wattie Creek they sat themselves down
Now it don't sound like much but it sure got tongues talking
Back at the homestead and then in the town

From little things big things grow
From little things big things grow

Vestey man said 'I'll double your wages
Seven quid a week you'll have in your hand'
Vincent said 'Uh-uh we're not talking about wages
We're sitting right here 'til we get our land'
Then Vestey man roared and Vestey man thundered
You don't stand the chance of a cinder in snow
Vince said 'If we fall others are rising'

From little things big things grow
From little things big things grow

Then Vincent Lingiarri boarded an aeroplane
Landed in Sydney, big city of lights
And daily he went round softly speaking his story
To all kinds of men from all walks of life

And Vincent sat down with big politicians
'This affair' they told him 'it's a matter of state
Let us sort it out, your people are hungry'
Vincent said 'No thanks, we know how to wait'

From little things big things grow
From little things big things grow

Then Vincent Lingiarri returned in an aeroplane
Back to his country once more to sit down
And he told his people 'Let the stars keep on turning
We have friends in the south, in the cities and towns'

Eight years went by, eight long years of waiting
'Til one day a tall stranger appeared in the land
And he came with lawyers and he came with great ceremony
And through Vincent's fingers poured a handful of sand

From little things big things grow
From little things big things grow

That was the story of Vincent Lingiarri
But this is the story of something much more
How power and privilege cannot move a people
Who know where they stand and stand in the law

From little things big things grow
From little things big things grow

BLUE STRANGER

Hello, blue stranger
Sitting there all alone
With your glass of sorrow you seem so far from home
Maybe you will let me buy a round or two
I'm a blue stranger too

Hello, blue stranger
I haven't seen you around
I know every reason for leaving town
We might know each other before this night is through
I'm a blue stranger too

And strangers fall in love every day
All lovers were strangers once, just like us
A little unsure of their way

Hello, blue stranger
Will you take a chance?
I might be mistaken but I see meaning in your glance
Maybe this could be the start of something new
I'm a blue stranger too

And strangers fall in love all the time
All lovers were strangers once, just like us
A little confused—sharing eyes

Yeah, strangers fall in love every night
All lovers were strangers once, just like us
Trying to get the words right

Hello, blue stranger
Hello, blue stranger
This one's on me

KEEP IT TO YOURSELF

I've been sleeping on my own
Ever since you've been away
You've been moving all around
You came home today
Maybe you've been with someone
You met after the show
Keep it to yourself
Keep it to yourself
Baby I don't want to know

If you're guilty in your heart
Just try and hold your tongue
If you want to let it out
Baby save it for a song
I don't want your honesty
Or descriptions blow by blow
Keep it to yourself
Keep it to yourself
Baby I don't want to know

Look around you! We're living in amazing times
They're not so important—your little crimes

I've been sleeping on my own
But I don't sleep all of the time
Twenty-four hours in one day
And sleeping's less than nine
There are many places in the sun
And many corners without you
Keep it to yourself
Keep it to yourself
And I'll keep my secrets too

INVISIBLE ME

Flying through the air tonight, way up in the sky
I can see lights below me as I'm passing by
Swooping down from cruising clouds, aiming for your street
Slipping through your window, moving with no feet

Invisible me
You might feel something brushing
It's only nothing
Just invisible me

Floating in the air tonight, high inside your room
And my eyes adjusting slowly to the gloom
Looking down I see a form and I know it's thee
Sleeping so softly but sleeping not with me

Invisible me
You might feel something rushing
It's only nothing
Just invisible me

LITTLE BOY DON'T LOSE YOUR BALLS

Little boy, you look so clear around the eyes
And what they've got in store for you you may not realise
So be careful when you hear the voices call
Watch out, little boy, don't lose your balls

'Cause you never know the rules until you play
First they stroke you then they screw you, try to take your
    balls away
And once they're gone they're way beyond recall
Watch out, little boy, don't lose your balls

Balls run wild
Balls may get way out of line
You may not even know you've left your balls way behind

You know money only buys you what you want
And you can't buy your balls back like you buy a pair of pants
And once they're gone you've really got fuck all
Watch out, little boy, don't lose your balls

BRAND NEW WAYS

I've been giving it all away
All my precious pearls to swine
You took my treasures and trashed them
I was blind
Now I've got to find
Some brand new ways

You've been taking it all around
Just like a little honey bee
You took your honey pot and jammed it
You did me wrong
Now the time has come
For brand new ways

Yes I heard your explanations
And I swallowed all your lies
I didn't know I could be so foolish
I never saw it in your eyes

I've been hanging on much too long
I've been dangling on a thin, thin thread
Well I'd be better off dead and buried
For all time
Unless I can find
Some brand new ways
Got to find
Some brand new ways

TREATY

WRITTEN WITH MANDAWUY YUNUPINGU

I heard it on the radio
I saw it on the television
Back in 1988
All those talking politicians

Words are easy, words are cheap
Much cheaper than our priceless land
And promises can disappear
Just like writing in the sand

Treaty, now
Treaty, yeah

This land was never given up
This land was never bought or sold
The planting of the Union Jack
Never changed our law at all

Now two rivers ran their course
Separated for so long
I'm dreaming of a brighter day
When the waters will be one

Treaty, now
Treaty, yeah

WHEN I FIRST MET YOUR MA

When I first met your mother
I was playing in a bar
She walked in with my girlfriend
My foolish girlfriend brought her there
She looked so pretty and dangerous
As she brushed back her hair
And I was not the only one
Taking notice in that bar
When I first met your ma

When I first kissed your mother
I was single once again
We walked through Fitzroy Gardens
There she took my hand
We could not stop our kissing
Then she whispered in my ear
'Soon you'll get to know me,
So let's not go too far'
When I first kissed your ma

Love like a bird flies away
You'll find out the only way
Love like a bird flies away

When we first lay together
Inside her father's house
We tried so to be quiet
As we held each other close
Then her dad came pounding and kicked me
    out of there
I walked two miles in Melbourne rain
I could have walked ten more
When I first loved your ma

Love like a bird flies away
You'll find out the only way
Love like a bird flies away

RALLY ROUND THE DRUM
WRITTEN WITH ARCHIE ROACH

Like my brother before me
I'm a tent boxing man
Like our daddy before us
Travelling all around Gippsland
I woke up one cold morning
Many miles from Fitzroy
And slowly it came dawning
By Billy Leach I was employed

Rally round the drum boys
Rally round the drum
Every day, every night boys
Rally round the drum

Hoisting tent pole and tarpaulin
Billy says 'Now beat the drum'
Rings out across the showgrounds
And all the country people come
Then Billy starts a-calling
'Step right up, step right up, one and all
Is there anybody game here
To take on Kid Snowball?'

Rally round the drum boys
Rally round the drum
Every day, every night boys
Rally round the drum

Sometimes I fight a gee-man
Yeah we put on a show
Sometimes I fight a hard man
Who wants to lay me low
Sometimes I get tired

But I don't ever grouse
I've got to keep on fighting
Five dollars every house

Rally round the drum boys
Rally round the drum
Every day, every night boys
Rally round the drum

Like my daddy before me
I stand up and knock 'em down
Like my brother before me
I'm weaving in your town

Yeah, rally round the drum boys
Rally round the drum
Got to keep on fighting
Rally round the drum

DON'T EXPLAIN

Don't explain
It's really not your style
I've had some fun
You really made me smile
Don't look so serious
It doesn't suit your face
Don't explain, don't explain

You sure know
How to use your hands
But you don't have a great attention span
Don't apologise
Or drop your eyes
Don't explain, don't explain

I've seen them come, I've seen them go
Boys like you
Their gangster hearts, their dreamy loads
Boys like you

So take your things
I won't count the days
Sure you can call on me
If you pass this way
But if one night you're lonely
And I have other company
Don't complain, don't complain

TAUGHT BY EXPERTS

You stand there looking so surprised
Sad confusion in your eyes
I know what you're going through
Oh baby I've been there too
And it hurts
I was taught by experts

You say I play a cheating game
I never keep the rules the same
I learned a thing or two
What I learned I learned from you
And it works
I was taught by experts

You put the weapon in my hand
You made me what I am

Now everything has turned around
Down is up and up is down
You got your fingers burned
Your little worm has turned
In the dirt
I was taught by experts
Don't it hurt
I was taught by experts

FOGGY HIGHWAY

I'm on a foggy highway
I'm on a lonely road
I can't see the way ahead
I'm on a foggy highway

Don't know just why I'm out here
Don't know just how I strayed
The road behind me is long and dark
I'm on a foggy highway

Cold my heart
Cold the ground
And my way is darkest night
Not a word
Not a friend
To help or guide me
To walk beside me tonight

I'm on a foggy highway
I'm on a lonely road
I'm not long for this world
I'm on a foggy highway

NOBODY SHE KNOWS
WRITTEN WITH GYAN

She leaves the house one morning
Long before the sun is shining
Imagines him waking alone in their bed
No message on the table
Just a half a cup of coffee
The paper upon the stairs still unread
At eight o'clock she's breathing just a little more easy
At ten o'clock she's many miles down the line

Now she's no one
Bound to no one
She's nobody she knows

At twelve o'clock she's dozing
Leaning on a perfect stranger
She wakes up to the sound of 'Show your tickets, please'
She smiles and says she's sorry
The stranger tells her not to worry
And offers her a coat to cover her knees
And all the empty stations pass by them in conversation
At four o'clock her gentleman bids her goodbye

Now she's no one
Bound to no one
She's nobody she knows

And as the shadows lengthen
Stretching to the far horizon
A voice starts calling
Keeps on calling
'You're no one
Bound to no one
You're nobody you know'

TEACH ME TONIGHT

I know I have a lot to learn
I am young, I've got love to burn
So take me by the hand
And show me how to read you right
Won't you teach me tonight?

I can tell by your eyes that you know
More than you ever like to show
Won't you take me to your room
And show me what's never seen the light?
Come on teach me tonight

I am just a boy who hasn't had much schooling
No no no no no no no
But I can learn fast, you won't catch me sleeping
No no no no no no no

Now I'm waiting for the class to begin
And I'm jumping right out of my skin
I'm standing at attention
I'm gonna study you with all my might
Won't you teach me tonight?
Come on teach me tonight

PLAY ME

Play me
Like the wind upon a leaf
Like a ripple on the sea
I want you to play me

Play me
Tonight I'm in your hands
I will follow your commands
So come on and play me

You're my only lover
You're my sweetest friend
When you take me over
The pleasure never ends

Play me
Like a bow upon a string
I begin to sing
Whenever you play me

Play me
Tonight we're heaven bound
Let the earth keep spinning round
We'll go on and on and on
Come on! Come on and play me

You're my only lover
You're my sweetest friend
When you take me over
The pleasure never ends

BETWEEN TWO SHORES

WRITTEN WITH VIKA AND LINDA BULL

Between two shores
My spirit soars
Between two shores
I will always be

Ever since I was a child
They didn't like me running wild
They had their plans set in stone
I had to get out on my own

Between two shores
My spirit soars
Between two shores
I will always be

When the winter rains came down
I nearly turned my head around
I was counting every day
But I knew I had to stay

Between two shores
My spirit soars
Between two shores
I will always be

They never treated me unkind
Still, you were always on my mind
I staked my claim, I found a place
But I never lost your face

Between two shores
My spirit soars
Between two shores
I will always be

THANKS I'LL THINK IT OVER
WRITTEN WITH VIKA AND LINDA BULL

Well your clothes are fine
And you drink good wine
You're a man of many powers
You have a big house on the hill
And lovely taste in flowers

Now you're calling me almost daily
You say you want no other
I don't mind this flattery
But thanks, I'll think it over

Oh give me ninety-nine years
Thanks, I'll think it over

What you want you always get
With just one snap of your fingers
But I have not decided yet
I know it makes you wonder

Oh give me ninety-nine years
Thanks, I'll think it over

Every day you're still calling me
From one place or another
Hold your horses, let me be!
Thanks, I'll think it over

Oh give me ninety-nine years
Thanks, I'll think it over

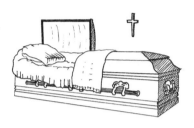

FUNERALS AND CIRCUSES

1992

Until Death Do Them Part
They Don't Have To Do My Dirty Job
Deadly
Do Right Man
Nobody Knows Nona
Never Never Never
I Am What I Am
Up Down In Out
The Tap Song
Jessie's Lullaby
Finale Song

UNTIL DEATH DO THEM PART

We are gathered here today to join a woman and a man
And to witness what they say as before us they stand
In sickness and in health, through the rich times and the poor
They are bound to be together and to live under God's law

Until death do them part
Or the stars fall from the sky
Until death do them part
And the rivers all run dry
What God has joined together
Let no one tear apart
They are bound to love each other
Until death do them part

We are gathered here today to join a husband and a wife
So I call on you to pray for good luck in their life
Through thick and through thin, through the good times
    and the bad
May they always be respectful and make each other glad

Until death do them part
When God calls from on high
Until death do them part
And it's time to say goodbye
What God has joined together
Let no one tear apart
They are bound to love each other
Until death do them part
Yes they are bound to be together
Until death do them part

THEY DON'T HAVE TO DO MY DIRTY JOB

Everybody's always got an opinion
They all know just how to run this town
I get it from the riff-raff, I get it from the snobs
They don't have to do my dirty job

Nobody much likes to be a copper
And no one wants to be a copper's friend
But suddenly I'm popular when someone gets robbed
They don't have to do my dirty job

All the boys are like their fathers
And all the girls are like their mothers

I'm always in a no-win situation
Though I try so hard to make things square
And old familiar faces can become an angry mob
They don't have to do my dirty job

All the girls are like their mothers
All the boys are like their fathers

Everybody's always on the right side
And every villain thinks that he's been framed
Everybody wants the lowdown but no one wants to dob
They don't have to do my dirty job

DEADLY

Pull the trigger fella, now come on and gun me down
I've been dead a hundred times but you can't put me in
   the ground
Every day I drink your poison, every day I bust your traps
So start shooting! Just like Rasputin—I'm deadly!

I've been bashed, I've been beaten, I've been buried alive
Left for dead inside your prison cell ten by five
They tried to break my spirit, put a blanket on my soul
Now I'm out of the hole—and I'm deadly!

I'm a critical mass I got a rocket in my pocket
I'm a livewire connection plugging into your socket
When you see me coming and you start to get the urge
Watch out! I'm a power surge—and I'm deadly!

I can drink more cans than any man can
Smoke more green than anybody's ever seen
I can eat a whole killer just put it on the table
I'm ready, willing and able—and I'm deadly!

I'm Tarzan, Batman, Attila the Hun
Alexander the Great all rolled up into one
Bullets bounce off me like rain off a tin roof
I'm a hundred percent proof—and I'm deadly!

DO RIGHT MAN

I'm a do right man and I'm walking tall
I'm a do right man with my back to the wall
I'm a do right man, I'm the one to call
I'm a do right man

I'm a do right man and I live by the law
I'm a do right man and my aim is sure
I'm a do right man knocking on your door
I'm a do right man

Do right, do right for you
You got trouble I'll help you through
Do right night and day
Well I'm here to stay
No I won't go away

I'm a do right man, yeah, I fight for my rights
I'm a do right man, got you in my sights
I'm a do right man, oooh! out go the lights
I'm a do right man

I'm a do right man and I walk the line
I'm a do right man, yeah, the straight shooting kind
I'm a do right man and I'm right on time
I'm a do right man

Do right, do right for you
You got trouble I'll help you through
Do right night and day
Yeah I'm here to stay
No I won't go away
I'm a do right man

NOBODY KNOWS NONA

Nobody knows Nona
Nobody knows Nona
I just want to get to know her
All I need's a little time

Nobody knows Nona
Nobody knows Nona
I think I'm gonna get to know her
I got myself a little time

I know she's fine like a mare running wild
And I know she loves me, she makes me feel like a child
And I know I love her so
Nobody knows Nona
Not even Nona knows

Nobody knows Nona
Nobody knows Nona
I hope I'm gonna get to know her
I got myself a little time

I know she's strong—she's got a mind of her own
And you can't tame her or turn her head back home
And I know she rolls and flows
Nobody knows Nona
Not even Nona knows

NEVER NEVER NEVER

There's a new emotion stirring me inside
To the surface from the darkness
I can feel it rise
A funny kind of feeling—it's scary and it's strange
I can't name it but I swear that
Everything has changed

And I've never, never, never felt quite like this before

Once this town was so big
Or maybe I was small
Now I see it and I know it's not so big at all

No I've never, never, never felt quite like this before

Well I'd call the doctor but I feel so good
A doctor won't help me at all
And I'd tell somebody but I don't know if I should
They won't listen to me, they won't listen
They don't listen at all

No I've never, never, never felt quite like this before

I AM WHAT I AM

I'm pleased to meet you
Let me shake you by the hand
I'm at your service
Your wish is my command
You do the right thing
You've got a friend
I mean what I'm saying
I am what I am

I'm straight as an arrow
What you see is what you get
I tell it how it is
And I ain't finished yet
I call a spade a spade
I call a gin a gin
I call a monkey a monkey
I am what I am

I never finished high school
It didn't set me back
I got the greatest little place here
This side of the black stump
I call a dog a dog
You know what I mean
I call a monkey a monkey
I am what I am

I don't pull my punches
I don't beat around the bush
I never start a fight
But I don't back off when I'm pushed
I call a spade a spade
I call a gin a gin
I call a monkey a monkey
I am what I am

UP DOWN IN OUT

It must go up before it comes down
That's what my grandma said to me
It must go up before it comes down
That's the way it has to be

Sir Isaac Newton lying on the ground
An apple fell and hit him on the crown
Up he jumped and shouted 'I have found the key
Every action has a reaction
And everybody has an attraction to every other body
It's called gravity'

Il faut monter avant de descendre
C'est ce que ma grandmère m'a dit
Il faut monter avant de descendre
Ça se passe toujours dans la vie

It must go in before it comes out
That's what my grandma said to me
It must go in before it comes out
That's the way it has to be

THE TAP SONG

Tap tap tap at my window
Tap tap tap at my pane
Just the wind and the rain again
Tap tap tap on my rooftop
Tap tap tap on my door
It's a song I've heard before
And it's the same old song
That I heard when I was young
Makes me feel so warm and sure
And when it all comes down
Wrap yourself up in that sound
Woman to woman
That's the score

JESSIE'S LULLABY

Sleep, Jessie, go to sleep
I will dry your eyes
The sun is going to rise
Sleep, Jessie, go to sleep
I will keep you warm
Safe from any harm

Dream, Jessie child, dream
I will keep you warm
Safe from any harm
Dream, Jessie child, dream
I will dry your eyes
The sun is going to rise

FINALE SONG

Up and down day by day
Round and round day by day

If happiness comes your way
Wear it lightly, friend
It may not last too long

If you're crying brother
Sister just hold on
You will find a new song

Up and down day by day
Round and round day by day

WANTED MAN
1994

Summer Rain
She's Rare
Just Like Animals
Love Never Runs On Time
Song From The Sixteenth Floor
Maybe This Time For Sure
Ball And Chain
You're Still Picking The Same Sore
Everybody Wants To Touch Me
We've Started A Fire
Lately
Nukkanya

Melbourne Girls
I Was Hoping You'd Say That
Cradle Of Love
I Didn't Know Love Could Be Mine
The Cake And The Candle
He Can't Decide
These Lies

SUMMER RAIN

She comes and goes like summer rain
I wait all day for summer rain
And when she comes I smile again
She cools my brain like summer rain

She'll change your plans like summer rain
I raise my arms to summer rain
I lift my head and taste again
The sweet, sweet drops of summer rain

She's warm, she's fresh like summer rain
She comes in a rush like summer rain
And when she comes she makes a change
I wait all day for summer rain

SHE'S RARE

Some men climb mountains just to test their soul
Other men dig down in the ground looking for buried gold
Some men go diving and never come up for air
I'm a climber, I'm a miner, I'm a diver for her
Because she's rare

Down at the track they're all standing in line
Out on the oval it's just three-quarter time
Inside the ring all you hear is a dull roar
I'm a gambler, I'm a player, I'm a fighter for her
Because she's rare, she's rare

There's a man with a gun on the lake before daylight
Another man dressed in black creeping round your door
   last night
And a man with a rod sitting on the end of the pier
I'm a hunter, I'm a thief, I'm a fisherman for her
Because she's rare, she's rare

Outside in the alley I can hear the deal go down
Over in the park another bottle's going round
Somebody's in trouble 'cause they can't cough up their share
I'm hanging out, I'm thirsty, I'm raging for her
Because she's rare, she's rare, so rare

JUST LIKE ANIMALS

It's a sunny Sunday but we don't want to get out of bed
So we unplug the telephone—we've got better things
    to do instead
There's no one home—nobody with a name

We're just like animals, just like animals
Rolling and tumbling on and on
Just like animals, just like animals
And her loving comes on so strong

It's a long, long Monday, working my fingers down to the bone
When I get a little minute I call her up on the telephone
She says hurry home, please hurry home

We're just like animals, just like animals
Rolling and tumbling on and on
Just like animals, just like animals
And her loving comes on so strong

Driving through the crosstown traffic
No matter how I try every single light turns to red
So I turn up the radio
And watch her dancing inside my head
She moves so fine, moves so fine

We're just like animals, just like animals
Rolling and tumbling on and on
Just like animals, just like animals
Yeah her loving comes on so strong

LOVE NEVER RUNS ON TIME

I pulled out of the suburbs by sunset
Rain was falling, it looked like it would for a while
I had a radio, a six-pack and some cigarettes
The radio died after the first hundred miles
I sang all the way to the border and guess who starred
    in every rhyme
Ah you know and I know that love never runs on time

I followed that old river 'til the morning
I stopped, I don't remember the name of the town
But the colour of the coffee was a warning
It was the colour of the river but not nearly as brown
The waitress poured me another, I guess she was feeling kind
You know and I know that love never runs on time

You're lost in the traffic
I've been asking around, but you haven't been seen
I never thought we were perfect
Oh but darling—what we could have been!

The rain came and went all the next day
I pulled over sometime for a sleep on the side
Then I gunned her back out on the highway
Hit a big pot-hole and the radio came alive
I never heard a love song yet that I could call yours and mine
'Cause you know and I know that love never runs on time

SONG FROM THE SIXTEENTH FLOOR

Something's frying on the floor below
I'm leaning out of my window
The sky's on fire, the street's all aglow
And somebody's singing to the radio
I would jump from the sixteenth floor
If I only could get next to you
Put my head in a lion's jaw if I only could get next to you
I'm walking the floor, I'm climbing the walls
I wake up from dreaming, that's when I fall
I would jump from the sixteenth floor
If I only could get next to you
Put my head in a lion's jaw if I only could get next to you
Over broken glass I would crawl, yes I would darling
Every day I speak your name
If I had wings I'd fly 'cause you're not here to hold me
I'd walk on burning coal, I'd sell my only soul
I would jump from the sixteenth floor, put my head
    in a lion's jaw
Take a ride on Niagara Falls if I only could get next to you

MAYBE THIS TIME FOR SURE

Maybe this time for sure
Things are gonna work out different
Not the way they did before
Maybe this time for sure
I can break out of the circle
I can find another door

Maybe this time I just might learn my lesson
Maybe this time I'll leave the past behind
Maybe this time I'll grab hold of my chances
Maybe this time I'll have a clearer mind

Maybe this time for sure
I can look into the mirror
I can stay up off the floor
Maybe this time for sure
I can roll right with the punches
I can hold some things in store

Maybe this time their tongues will all fall silent
Maybe this time I'll make them eat their words
Maybe this time I'll listen to the warnings
Maybe this time I'll hold onto my nerve

Maybe this time for sure
I'll keep both my eyes wide open
I'll know what I'm living for
Maybe this time for sure
I can walk the straight and narrow
On the right side of the law

Maybe this time I'll stick with my intentions
Maybe this time I'll have no need to lie
Maybe this time I won't fall for temptation
Maybe this time Satan will pass me by

BALL AND CHAIN

I think about you, baby, think about you all the time
No matter what I do you know you're never really
  off of my mind
But I got trouble here, nobody's cutting me any slack
And every day I stay the knives are getting closer to my back

I'm gone! So long!
It's driving me right out of my brain
Oh I'm never gonna be your ball and chain

When I first came to town, well, everybody shook me
  by the hand
I flashed it all around, everywhere I turned I had a friend
Oh I got stitched, now things are tearing at the seams
But you've stuck by me, baby, you take away bad dreams

I'm sad! Too bad!
It's driving me right out of my brain
'Cause I'm never gonna be your ball and chain

I think about you, baby, think about the days ahead
I know it won't be long before somebody else is in your bed
I gotta keep moving, something's just about to break
And I won't forget the way you move like a swan on a lake

I'm gone! So long!
It's driving me right out of my brain
I'm never gonna be your ball and chain

YOU'RE STILL PICKING THE SAME SORE

I have known you both now it seems for so long
I can't get you together so I've written you a song
Take it as you please with a frown or with a smile
Or think about it for a while
You're still fighting an old, old war
You just keep on picking the same sore

First I hear one story like it's the cold hard facts
Then I hear the other say 'No, it was never like that'
One day I'm a doctor, the next day I'm a guide
And you both want me to take sides
You're still fighting a cold, cold war
And you just keep on picking the same sore

No matter what I do I know that I can't win
He says 'What'd she say?' then she says 'What'd you hear
   from him?'
And neither one of you will ever take the blame
You both should be ashamed
When you first met you were just like kids in a candy store
Now you both keep picking the same sore

I think I'll get together all your friends and me
And we'll buy a boat and send you off to sea
And you can sail that ship to a far off distant shore
And keep on fighting evermore
And there'll be no one there for you to bore
And you can both keep picking the same sore

EVERYBODY WANTS TO TOUCH ME

Everybody wants to touch me
Everybody wants a feel
Everybody wants a piece of something that's real

Everybody wants to touch me
They all love my skin
They all want to take me home
They don't even care where I've been

Everybody wants to touch me
Everybody wants a little pat
They can't wait to tell their friends
How they had themselves a piece of that

Everybody wants to touch me
Everybody wants to touch me
Everybody wants to touch me
Everybody wants to touch me

Everybody's lost their manners
Everybody's in a rush
One starts to push, another starts to shove
Then they all get caught in the crush

Everybody wants to touch me
Everybody wants a slice
Everybody wants to touch me
Want a little magic in their lives

WE'VE STARTED A FIRE

Morning is rising
Suddenly I open my eyes
Sun don't catch me
Lying here by your side
We're like two children playing with matches
Hidden from the world

We've started a fire
We've started a fire
We've started a fire
We can't put out

Kiss me, then let me go before the sun is high
Once kiss—one spark!
Danger when the powder is dry
We're just two children playing with matches
Hidden from the world

We've started a fire
We've started a fire
We've started a fire
We can't put out

Morning is rising
Lying here by your side
Daylight comes shining, burning right into my eyes
We're just like children playing with matches
Hidden from the world

We've started a fire
We've started a fire
We've started a fire
We can't put out

LATELY

WRITTEN WITH RENEE GEYER

Lately I must have changed
All day long I'm dreaming
Lately I lose my way
When I'm running some small errand
Maybe I'm lucky some people are kind
Lately you've been on my mind

It's funny what gets disregarded
Right before your eyes
It's funny how everybody else can see it
And you're the last to realise
A secret spell has caught me in the sweetest bind
Lately you've been on my mind

I had almost forgotten
The way it used to feel
From a sleep I've woken
Now the dream is real

Lately I don't take for granted
Every moment passing by
Lately I'm trapped in wonder
When you move I'm mesmerised
You have blessed me, you've made me shine
Lately you've been on my mind

NUKKANYA

Outside the dogs are barking
And the morning sun is breaking through the trees
My heart is feeling heavy
As I listen to the moaning of the breeze
Nukkanya, baby, I really don't want to leave

There's a ticket in my pocket
I'd toss it if I only had my way
And a suitcase in the hallway
I wish I could unpack it now and stay
Nukkanya, baby, I'm gonna be back some day

Nukkanya
Don't it go to show what a man don't know
Nukkanya
Nukkanya, baby, I really don't want to go

My land was once a river
I hate to see it slowly bleeding dry
My love is like an eagle
High across the valleys she will fly
Nukkanya, baby, I'll see you by and by

Nukkanya
Don't it go to show what a man don't know
Nukkanya
Nukkanya, baby, I really don't want to go

MELBOURNE GIRLS

I heard the news, come sit right down
You lost out this time round
I've got a bottle that I've been saving
Let's talk these things over
And I won't try to cheer you up
I've drunk from that same cup
Now I've got a bottle that'll last all night
Let's drink 'til we're sober

Another crash landing
But we're still standing
And we will survive
Melbourne girls don't cry

I have tried to work things out
The more I know the more I doubt
But this I know—we'll still be here
When all this is over

Another crash landing
But we're still standing
And we will survive
Melbourne girls don't cry

I WAS HOPING YOU'D SAY THAT

You were a flash of white riding past on a bike
Your sunglasses a long streak of black
I called out 'Hello', you said 'Hello yourself'
I was hoping you'd say that

You stopped up the block at a café I knew
Outside at a table you sat
I said 'Can I join you?' You said 'If you like'
I was hoping you'd say that

I was hoping you'd say that
I was hoping you would
I was hoping you'd say that
When you did it did me good

I gave you my number, you gave me yours
I called you then you called me back
I said 'You like the movies?' You said 'Sure I do'
I was hoping you'd say that

The movie was dumb, the plot was a joke
The hero was caught in a trap
When he made his big stand you grabbed hold of my hand
I was hoping you'd do that

I was hoping you'd do that
I was hoping you would
I was hoping you'd do that
When you did, it felt pretty good

After the film I drove you home
We talked for a minute on your step
You said 'Would you like to come in for a while?'
I was hoping you'd say that

You put on some music and rolled up a smoke
I started to feel relaxed
You said 'Do you feel like lying down?'
I was hoping you'd say that
I was hoping you'd say that
I was hoping you'd say that

CRADLE OF LOVE

Baby, you look tired, baby, you look beat
Seems like you've been working eight days a week
Baby, take a break from all you're thinking of
And come into my cradle of love

Baby, let me hold you and rock your cares away
Put aside your troubles at the ending of the day
'Cause when we lie together I fit you like a glove
Come into my cradle of love

Down in the valley you can lose your name
Your sorrow and your pain
The dark, warm waters can heal you
And make you clean again

So, baby, come on over and lean your head on me
Here in my arms now is where you're meant to be
Baby, take advantage of all I've got to give
And let me be your cradle of love

I DIDN'T KNOW LOVE COULD BE MINE

Lightning has struck with a name
I'm burned and I'll never be the same
My wires are crossed, I'm open to secrets and signs
Oh I didn't know love could be mine

Thunder has brought blessed rain
My rivers are running untamed
Every inch of the land has suddenly come alive
Oh I didn't know love could be mine

I was blind—now I see
I was lame
Then you touched me
You touched me so fine

You made the dumb shout and sing
You gave a prisoner wings
You healed the sick, you turned the water into wine
Out of the blue you came
I never dreamed I could change
Now yesterday seems such a long way behind
Oh I didn't know love could be mine

I was blind—now I see
I was lame
Then you touched me
And I came alive
I didn't know love could be mine

THE CAKE AND THE CANDLE

I don't ask much
Only what's mine
I know just what I'm worth
I'll get what I deserve
Look at me now
I'm in my prime
My eyes are on the prize
There'll be no compromise this time
You can still change your mind
If this is more than you can handle
'Cause I want it all, that's what I'm here for
I want the cake
I want the candle

You've had your share
Of pleasure and pain
All that was just a taste
Before the feast
So bring me your body
Bring me your flame
I'll make you burn so bright
I'll make you shout my name
You can still change your mind
If you can't afford the scandal
Yeah I want it all
Body and soul
I want the cake
And I want the candle
I want the whole damn cake and candle

HE CAN'T DECIDE

HIM:

I love her my long, tall woman
I love her my little, short woman
I love her my middle-size woman
But I can't decide
Now each time that we're together
One by one they ask me whether
I love one more than the other
But I can't decide

LONG TALL WOMAN:

A long, tall mama is a mighty good lover
And you never have to worry when she moans
When you're rockin' and a-ridin' and a-slippin' and a-slidin'
You're never gonna break her bones
And a long, tall mama is a mighty good cover
When the temperature is way down low
And it's well to remember she's much cooler in the summer
There's a breeze everywhere she goes

HIM:

I love her my long, tall woman
I love her my little, short woman
I love her my middle-size woman
But I can't decide
Now each time that we're together
One by one they ask me whether
I love one more than the other
But I can't decide

LITTLE SHORT WOMAN:

A little, short mama is a treasure to discover
And she always makes a man feel tall

With her sweet disposition she won't make an exhibition
Of herself to every Peter and Paul
A little, short mama is a pocketful of pleasure
And she knows a hundred different ways
She's small enough to study every square inch of your body
And her tongue is always full of praise

HIM:
I love her my little, short woman
I love her my long, tall woman
I love her my middle-size woman
But I can't decide
Now each time that we're together
One by one they ask me whether
I love one more than the other
But I can't decide

MIDDLE-SIZE WOMAN:
A middle-size mama is a just right mama
You can look her squarely in the eye
And it's always perfect weather every minute that you're with her
You never feel the time go by
And she's never too hard and she's never too soft
You fit her like a finger in a glove
And you're closest to perfection when she's giving you affection
It's her you're always thinking of

HIM:
I love her my middle-size woman
I love her my little, short woman
I love her my long, tall woman
But I can't decide

THEM:
Now what shall we do with this brother?
Why should we wait at his pleasure?

Let's put all our heads together
If he can't decide
We know what to do with this brother
Send him back home to his mother
'Cause we can get plenty of other
And he can't decide

THESE LIES

WRITTEN WITH DEBORAH BYRNE

Grandpa was a loving man
He sat me on his knee
I remember how he'd brush my hair so tenderly
A fortunate and loving man
He whispered in my ear
This secret's just between us when no one else is near

These lies brighter than sunlight
Fairytales told in a dream
These old lies in a bedtime story
These lies have covered me

Summer's sweet and budding fruit
Lies withered on the vine
And winter's icy fingers have stolen what was mine
The stars are shining high above the snow upon the ground
Hold me close and let me know that new love comes around

These lies brighter than sunlight
Fairytales told in a dream
These old lies in a bedtime story
These lies have covered me

DEEPER WATER

1996

Blush
Extra Mile
I'll Forgive But I Won't Forget
Deeper Water
Madeleine's Song
Difficult Woman
Give In To My Love
I've Been A Fool
Anastasia Changes Her Mind
California
Gathering Storm

Close
Summer Winter Spring And Fall
We'll Get Over It Somehow
Behind The Bowler's Arm
Mama Shake That Thing
Between Two Shores (Second Version)
How To Make Gravy

Our Sunshine
Perfect World
Killer Lover

BLUSH

She walks by the Indian Ocean
As the sun sinks in the west
From the beach a breeze is blowing
Playing with her cotton dress

All I want, I confess
I just want to see her blush

When we kiss she tastes so salty
On her cheek and on her neck
I can't wait 'til I get with her
So I can kiss her salty breasts

All I want, I confess
I just want to see her blush

In her room there's a little window
With a view right down to the shore
When night falls she lights a candle
Oh her skin's a coat of fire!

All I want, I confess
I just want to see her blush
I just want to see her blush
All across her chest
Take off her cotton dress
I just want to see her blush

EXTRA MILE

Just like the bee comes to the honey
You're swarming all over me
Now you got this close, eyes on the treasure
But it don't come for free
Can you go the extra mile?

So you want to jump into the ocean
Baby it's sink or swim
Can you keep your head up above the water
When the waves come crashing in?
Can you go the extra mile?

Can you stand the heat cooking in my kitchen?
Can you see this whole thing through?
Can you stand to get your hands all dirty?
That's what I want from you
Can you go the extra mile?
Can you go the extra mile?

I'LL FORGIVE BUT I WON'T FORGET

Sometimes the very best of friends just have to disagree
I've seen the very best of friends part forever bitter company
And you and I, we've had our share of ups and downs
But we've seen each other through
Though I have to say I always thought I was a better friend
    than you
You've let me down in so many little ways
You apologise and I always accept
'Cause I forgive but I don't forget

When you were hurt I took your pain, yeah I soaked up
    all your rage
And there were times you did the same for me, though you
    always complained
When all the others wrote you off I defended you, I stuck
    with you like glue
You're so generous and so completely selfish and I always
    kind of liked that about you
But this is one too many times you've treated me like
    a doormat
Oh I'll forgive but I won't forget

Dying comes at any time, living has no rules
Forgiving may get you favours but forgetting's just for fools

I can't believe she fucked you here and then fed me full of lies
Why don't I go and get her now
And you can fuck her again right before my eyes
Then you two can have each other
You deserve each other I bet
And I'll forgive but I won't forget
I won't forget
I'll forgive but I won't forget

DEEPER WATER

On a crowded beach in a distant time
At the height of summer see a boy of five
At the water's edge so nimble and free
Jumping over the ripples looking way out to sea

Now a man comes up from amongst the throng
Takes the young boy's hand and his hand is strong
And the child feels safe, yeah the child feels brave
As he's carried in those arms up and over the waves

Deeper water, deeper water, deeper water, calling them on

Let's move forward now and the child's seventeen
With a girl in the back seat tugging at his jeans
And she knows what she wants, she guides with her hand
As a voice cries inside him—I'm a man, I'm a man!

Deeper water, deeper water, deeper water, calling him on

Now the man meets a woman unlike all the rest
He doesn't know it yet but he's out of his depth
And he thinks he can run, it's a matter of pride
But he keeps coming back like a cork on the tide

Well the years hurry by and the woman loves the man
Then one night in the dark she grabs hold of his hand
Says 'There, can you feel it kicking inside!'
And the man gets a shiver right up and down his spine

Deeper water, deeper water, deeper water, calling them on

So the clock moves around and the child is a joy
But Death doesn't care just who it destroys

Now the woman gets sick, thins down to the bone
She says 'Where I'm going next, I'm going alone'

On a distant beach, lonely and wild
At a later time, see a man and a child
And the man takes the child up into his arms
Takes her over the breakers
To where the water is calm

Deeper water, deeper water, deeper water, calling them on

MADELEINE'S SONG

When I dream at night it's you I see walking
And in the dream I hear you laughing and talking
When I'm all alone it's you that I'm missing
When I think of fun it's you that I'm kissing
My sweet Madeleine, my sweet Madeleine
My, my Madeleine, you never let me sleep

One of these old days you'll have yourself a boyfriend
But you'll always know my love will never end
When you cry so hard I wish you'd stop sobbing
You're gonna grow up soon and just want to go shopping
My sweet Madeleine, my sweet Madeleine
My, my Madeleine, you never let me sleep

DIFFICULT WOMAN

A difficult woman
Sometimes hurts her friends when she don't mean to
A difficult woman
Makes it hard for the ones she loves
It's easy to do
She's had to be tough all of her life
So she's built herself a wall
She doesn't know how to trust herself
So it's hard for her to trust at all
A difficult woman needs a special kind of friend

A difficult woman
Swings between shame and pride
A difficult woman
Has strong, strong stuff deep inside
And getting to her is no easy affair
It's like working in a mine
You'd better prepare to pay the price
If it's treasure you want to find
A difficult woman needs a special kind of friend

And living with her is better and worse
Than living with anyone else
She can be cruel or so kind
Oh you go from heaven to hell
If she got what she wanted
If she got what she needed
She wouldn't be hard to understand
A difficult woman needs a special kind of man

GIVE IN TO MY LOVE

Have you heard the news of my love?
Did they send a message down
That I'm on the march with my love?
And I'm death or glory bound
From the mountains to the marshes
My love is gaining ground
Give in to my love, give in to my love

Well I want to show you my love
It's bigger than a Cadillac
But you keep up your resistance
And you try to drive me back
I want to show you all my love
It's bigger than a Cadillac
Give in to my love, give in to my love

My love is like a drunkard
Holding up the bar
And he'll say the same thing over
And he'll fix you with his stare
You try and change the subject
But you won't escape the war
Give in to my love, give in to my love
Give in to my love, give in to my love

I'VE BEEN A FOOL

So you want a second chance
You want to start again, make everything alright
But I want to know if you've changed this time
Baby don't lie, don't you lie to me
What do you take me for?
I've been a fool, anyone can see
But I'll be your fool no more

You've got a way of talking
You could sell a poor man a bottle of air
But I want to know if you've changed at all
Baby don't lie, don't you lie to me
I've heard it all before
I've been a fool, most definitely
But I'll be your fool no more

Everybody loves you, I still love you
I want you back, I need you now
But I want to know
Have you changed your spots at all?
Baby don't lie, baby don't lie
I've been a fool, I've been a fool

ANASTASIA CHANGES HER MIND

Anastasia left a kiss on the mirror
And a couple of condoms by the bed
I tried to find her on her old number
But I just got her boyfriend instead
Oh it's hard, so hard
When Anastasia changes her mind

So I went back to working the quadrellas
I collected three times in a row
I swear it must have been that kiss on the mirror
That I'd touch with my lips just for luck each time I'd go
Oh it's hard, very hard
When Anastasia changes her mind

Now the numbers were my daily devotion
I was stashing big bills in the floor
Then one night at my door a commotion
Anastasia—at some ungodly hour!
I said 'Baby can I fix you a coffee
And tomorrow let me buy you a dress
Since you've been gone I got lucky'
She just nodded her head and said 'I guess'
Oh it's hard, yeah it's hard
When Anastasia changes her mind

Now 'Stacey' takes the crumbs from the table
And feeds them out back to the birds
Me, I can't even pick the daily double
Since that kiss on the mirror disappeared
Yeah it's hard, ain't it hard
When Anastasia changes her mind

CALIFORNIA

California—I can taste you even now
California—I'll get back to you somehow
I still see you in my dreams
I hear your name on every tongue
It's been so long

California—You whispered to me all last night
California—With your beauty like a knife
I can hear your siren song
Calling me back to your shore
To die once more, California

California—I took my story to the well
California—You're still eating at my soul
How I miss your greedy eyes
Our golden days, our purple nights
I'll pay the price, oooh California

GATHERING STORM

I had a dream
I saw you walking down the road
In a gathering storm

Wind on the rise
A black crow was flying
You alone in a gathering storm

I wake up alone in my bed
There's nothing before my eyes
And outside the door
Only the sighing
And you out there in a gathering storm

So cover your head
Keep your eyes open
Make speed in the gathering storm

I rise up and turn on the light
Now it's shining in my window
My walls are strong
My chimney's smoking
God speed you
In the gathering storm

CLOSE

WRITTEN WITH RENEE GEYER

This party's going down
I don't want to hang around here anymore
You've been leaning against the wall
Now I see you stalling somewhere at the door
Maybe you're thinking too
I wonder if I'm getting through to you
Take a walk across the floor
Baby let's get close
Take another look at me
Don't you want to get close

So we're riding in a taxi
Now we can relax just a little bit more
You're talking to me
I can only hear the sound of your voice and that's all
You put your hand on mine
You know I don't mind at all
Slide across the seat
Baby let's get close
I don't care, I don't care how close

Now I hold you in my arms
The world is far away behind the door
I feel every single hair on my body
Rise from each and every pore
I want to swim with you
Toss and turn and wash up on the shore
Come on, come on
Like a warm summer breeze on my face
So close

SUMMER WINTER SPRING AND FALL

WRITTEN WITH RENEE GEYER

Summer, winter, spring and fall
That's what you are to me
Four seasons in one day and more
Baby, you're a natural mystery
Your smile is the sun after the rain
You frown—the storm's back again

Summer, winter, spring and fall
Every day's brand new
I feel you stirring by my side
And I know just what to do
Your kiss is the heat of the sun
How I fall when you're gone

I'll drink while the river is high
Who knows when the river runs dry

WE'LL GET OVER IT SOMEHOW

You hit town like a cyclone
We thought we were prepared
For days the lines were buzzing
There was tension in the air
And everywhere you showed your face
You started up a row
Now everything is shattered
We'll get over it somehow

You circled and you twisted
Through each and every home
You cleaned us out completely
Stripped us to the bone
We never got our sights on you
Our eyes are open now
We're still picking up the pieces
We'll get over it somehow

You're flying all alone
Spinning out of control
And I do fear
The centre cannot hold

I'm so disappointed
That another good one's gone
You had power, grace and beauty
Something just went wrong
I have no more time to waste
Some things I won't allow
Don't try to make it better
I'll get over it somehow

BEHIND THE BOWLER'S ARM

Oh it's been a hard, hard year
Pushing shit uphill
But shit happens all the time
And I guess it always will
Now the days are getting long
Summer's on its way
And I can't wait for Christmas
'Cause the day after Christmas is Boxing Day
And you'll know where to find me
Ten rows back at the MCG
Right behind the bowler's arm

So leave your worries at the farm
Don't fret about the rain
Hold your credit over at the store
Bring the kids down on the train
Meet me on the Richmond side
Just outside the gate
I want to see that very first ball
But don't sweat if you're running late
'Cause you'll know where to find me
There's no other place I'd rather be
But right behind the bowler's arm

And if we're lucky we might see
Someone make a ton or a slashing fifty
Yeah if we're lucky there might be
A bowling spell of sheer wizardry
But most probably
Nothing much will happen at all

And when the angels add my days
And say my time is up

I'll say to them 'Now hold on please
There's just one thing that you forgot
I know each man must leave this world
Behind when he gets called
But we had a deal that you won't count
The days I watched the bat and the ball'
And the angels . . .
They'll know where to find me
There's no other place I'd rather be
But right behind the bowler's arm
Yeah they'll know where to find me
Ten rows back with sunburnt knees
Right behind the bowler's arm

MAMA SHAKE THAT THING

WRITTEN WITH VIKA AND LINDA BULL

The time has come my friend
To take you by the hand
You've been moping round, your mouth so down
C'mon girl, we're going to hit the town
Mama, mama, mama, shake that thing

Do you remember when
Every head would turn
The way you moved across the floor
You had it all, who could ask for more?
Mama, mama, mama, shake that thing

You taught me how to live
You dragged me into love
Well I can't stand to lose my friend
Now the wheel is turning, it's time to live again
Mama, mama, mama, shake that thing

BETWEEN TWO SHORES (SECOND VERSION)

WRITTEN WITH VIKA AND LINDA BULL

I have another place, so very far away
In dreams I'm always walking by the sea
No shoes upon my feet
Strong sun upon my back
I wake up and you're there right next to me

I left my childhood home
I came here on my own
The winter rains they chilled me through and through
And all the different ways, the very air was strange
I would have turned around if not for you
I will always be between two shores

This place is now my home
Our children here have grown
I would have turned around
If not for you

HOW TO MAKE GRAVY

Hello, Dan, it's Joe here, I hope you're keeping well
It's the twenty-first of December, and now they're ringing
   the last bells
If I get good behaviour, I'll be out of here by July
Won't you kiss my kids on Christmas Day, please don't
   let 'em cry for me
I guess the brothers are driving down from Queensland
Stella's flying in from the coast
They say it's gonna be a hundred degrees, even more maybe
   but that won't stop the roast
Who's gonna make the gravy now? I bet it won't taste the same
Just add flour, salt, a little red wine and don't forget a dollop
   of tomato sauce for sweetness and that extra tang
And give my love to Angus and to Frank and Dolly
Tell 'em all I'm sorry I screwed up this time
And look after Rita, I'll be thinking of her early
   Christmas morning
When I'm standing in line

I hear Mary's got a new boyfriend, I hope he can hold his own
Do you remember the last one? What was his name again?
(Just a little too much cologne)
And Roger, you know I'm even gonna miss Roger
'Cause there's sure as hell no one in here I want to fight
Oh praise the Baby Jesus, have a Merry Christmas
I'm really gonna miss it, all the treasure and the trash
And later in the evening, I can just imagine
You'll put on Junior Murvin and push the tables back
And you'll dance with Rita, I know you really like her
Just don't hold her too close, oh brother please don't stab me
   in the back
I didn't mean to say that, it's just my mind it plays up
Multiplies each matter, turns imagination into fact

You know I love her badly, she's the one to save me
I'm gonna make some gravy, I'm gonna taste the fat
Tell her that I'm sorry, yeah I love her badly, tell 'em all
    I'm sorry
And kiss the sleepy children for me
You know one of these days, I'll be making gravy
I'll be making plenty, I'm gonna pay 'em all back

OUR SUNSHINE

WRITTEN WITH MICHAEL THOMAS

There came a man on a stolen horse
And he rode right onto the page
Burning bright but not for long
Lit up with a holy rage
No turning back for the child of grace
With the blood red on his hand
Never known to hurt a woman
He never robbed an honest man
His mother held in jail, his daddy dead
And daily rising the price upon his head

Our sunshine, our sunshine
Through fire and flood, through tears and blood
Through dust and mud still riding on

Forever trapped in a suit of steel
With the hotel burning behind
Betrayed by his companions
And the train waiting down the line
Forever tall on a bareback horse
Getting through by the skin of his teeth
It's one more for the ladies
Now one more for the police
Riding all night hungry, tired and cold
Into the misty morning
He'll never grow old

Our sunshine, our sunshine
Through fire and flood, through tears and blood
Through dust and mud still riding on

As he stood before the judges chair
He said 'I'm free and easy—I'll see you there!'

Our sunshine, our sunshine
Through fire and flood, through tears and blood
Through dust and mud still riding on

PERFECT WORLD

WRITTEN WITH MICHAEL THOMAS

In a perfect world
I'd wake up with a clear head
You beside me in the bed
I'd rise up from my dreaming
To bless the brand new day
You would still be sleeping
I'd sneak out to the kitchen
To make some toast and coffee
Bring it to you on a tray
In a perfect world

In a perfect world
You'd rub your eyes and wake up
Smile at me and take the cup
Blow the steam off from the top
Take a sip and put it down
You'd shift your body in the bed
Put your arms around my head
And say the things that no one says
When others are around
In a perfect world

Last night I was drinking late
With someone who called me mate
He was paying so I stayed
Right up to closing time
I don't remember much at all
'Cept pissing up against a wall
And throwing up inside the hall
As soon as I got home
Such a perfect world

KILLER LOVER

I hear the key turning in the door
And then the footsteps creeping across the floor
Somebody's coming across the gloom
My assassin is in the room

(You, my killer lover)

My heart is hammering in its case
I feel your breath hot upon my face
Smiling murder in your eyes
Tonight there'll be no alibis

(You, my killer lover)

I die just a little when you touch my skin
Like the man in the bible I rise again
And when the sun beats in upon our eyes
I die once more before I rise

(You, my killer lover)

WORDS AND MUSIC
1998

Little Kings
I'll Be Your Lover Now
Nothing On My Mind
Words And Music
Gutless Wonder
Tease Me
I'd Rather Go Blind
She Answers The Sun (Lazybones)
Beat Of Your Heart
Glory Be To God
Saturday Night And Sunday Morning
Charlie Owen's Slide Guitar
Melting

Would You Be My Friend?
You Broke A Beautiful Thing
Last Night I Lay Dreaming
High Wild Ways
I Wasted Time
Whistling Bird

Let Me In
Be Careful What You Pray For
If I Could Start Today Again

LITTLE KINGS

I'm so afraid for my country
There's an ill wind blowing no good
So many lies in the name of history
They want to improve my neighbourhood

I'm so worried about my brother
He just gets sadder every day
We gotta take care of each other
Or else we're gonna have to pay

In the land of the little kings
There's a price on everything
And everywhere the little kings
Are getting away with murder

I was born in a lucky country
Every day I hear the warning bells
They're so busy building palaces
They don't see the poison in the wells

In the land of the little kings
Profit is the only thing
And everywhere the little kings
Are getting away with murder

In the land of the little kings
Justice don't mean a thing
And everywhere the little kings
Are getting away with murder

I'LL BE YOUR LOVER NOW

The fix is in, we should have known
It was always there from the start
Deep within, so slow and strong
Working its way to the heart
One day you notice a change
And then nothing's the same
I'll be your lover now, baby don't deny it
I'll be your lover now, money couldn't buy this

You crossed your mouth to keep mine shut
My timing was never that good
But I couldn't stand to see you mixed up
With a faker who kept his cards hid
I stayed in the game 'til the end
Waiting for my big hand
I'll be your lover now, money couldn't buy this
I'll be your lover now, baby don't deny it

'Cause I know your deep dirty places of pain
You know your secrets will always be safe
I'll keep them with mine, we're two of a kind
I'll be your lover now

The penny drops, the bottle spins
The stars all shift, the tables turn
The arrow strikes, the die is cast
The high shall be low and the first shall be last
I stayed in the game 'til the end
Waiting for my big hand
I'll be your lover now
You know your secrets will always be safe
Because there's nothing more precious than shame
I'll keep yours with mine, we're two of a kind
I'll be your lover now

NOTHING ON MY MIND

Rack 'em up Jim, it's your break
Set 'em up Max, it's my shout
You know I really could go a round or three
You wouldn't believe the crap I've had to deal with this week
And I'm shovelling most of it for free
'Grace under pressure'—that's what the old man said
Yeah the old man said a lot of things in his time
Well, fighting a bull's one thing but fighting bullshit's another
And around here you know the bullshit just never seems to die
I just want nothing on my mind

Christ hell! It's warming up in here, listen to that guitar player
    will ya
Do you think anyone could get him to turn down?
Where'd Jim go, sorry I didn't catch your name
It's impossible to hear a word above that sound
I'm a little thirsty, I'm running out of money, hey I'm a legend
    not a star
And I'll talk to anyone yes I will
Just as long as I can keep ripping the scab off those cold little
    vicious ones as they keep coming right across the bar
I just want nothing on my mind

There was a man on the radio today talking about
    the young people
Said we should listen to the young people, said they're a victim
    of conspiracy
The young people, Jesus! What's that supposed to mean?
I never did one damn good thing 'til I was over thirty
I'm gonna get up in the morning, chug-a-lug a coffee
Get on my bike and ride away
Find me a beach with a nice little break and I'm gonna catch
    wave after wave after wave
Until there's nothing on my mind
(Whoever brought me here will have to take me home)

WORDS AND MUSIC

I was standing in the schoolyard
I guess it was sometime in 1965
Just me and my friends listening to the radio
And a song came on called I Feel Fine
The playground sounds grew dim
The whole wide world seemed to fade
There was nothing but me and that heavenly sound
Burning in my brain
Words and music—yeah, yeah

I was lying on the living room floor
With the sound way up on Highway 61
Then I heard my mother calling through the door
Saying 'Now, what about those dishes then, son?'
So I picked the needle up
And yelled out 'Just one more song to go'
Then I put the needle back down
At the start of Desolation Row
Words and music—yeah, yeah

Now two things saved that crazy sailor
Trapped for days inside his hull
No food, no water, no nothing
Just his tongue rattling around inside his skull
Words and music—yeah, yeah

GUTLESS WONDER

Here he comes now, gutless wonder, with his merry crew
Stepping lightly, smiling brightly, those big eyes on you
Bet your bottom dollar he will talk you up
Bet your bottom dollar he will sweep you up
He's a nimble fella, better watch your step
With the old soft shoe
Bet your bottom dollar he will suck your prick
Bet your bottom dollar he will make it slick
He's a rubber fella with a mean back flip
When you're out of view

Gutless wonder, dancing around you, almost cheek to cheek
Smell his hunger, feel his power, it can make you weak
Bet your bottom dollar he will suck your prick
Bet your bottom dollar he will make it slick
He's a double fella with a mean back flip
And a smooth soft shoe
Bet your bottom dollar he will lap it up
Bet your bottom dollar you won't fill him up
He's an empty fella, watch him swelling up
He's got the drip on you
He's got the grip on you

Here he comes, watch out now!
Gutless wonder on the prowl!
Watch your step, he's a gaping hole
Gutless wonder will suck your soul

TEASE ME

I know that I look kinda funny
Sometimes I just don't act right
I'm not a teenage dream, I never made the team
Like Frankenstein I give some people a fright
I don't even have to try
They cross the street to pass me by

I like this place it's noisy
I like it when the light's down low
Now Candy sure looks fine and Honey's kinda wild
But you're the one that really steals the show
I swear you looked into my eyes
Oh I'll love you 'til the day you die

C'mon tease me, c'mon tease me, baby
C'mon tease me, I can take it, baby

I'd like to take you somewhere with no one else around
If it was just me and you, imagine what I'd do
Nobody there to ever hear a sound
I could change your pretty face
Oh, my beauty, don't you need the beast

C'mon tease me, c'mon tease me, baby
C'mon tease me, I can take it, baby

It's oh so late, it's too late to care
Time gentlemen please
I'll have one scotch, one bourbon, one beer
Please don't let the music stop
'Cause you know, baby, what it is that you got
You don't even have to try
Oh I'll love you 'til the day you die

C'mon tease me, c'mon tease me, baby
C'mon tease me, I can take it, baby

I'D RATHER GO BLIND

I suppose I should get over this
I'm not the first and not the last
To ever wake up with a hurt inside
But it just won't go away
It's getting worse now every day
And I can't find a hole that's big enough for me
    to crawl and hide
I'd rather go blind, I'd rather go blind
Than see you with another guy

You made a special tape for me
With songs from all your favourite CDs
I put it on today then I had to turn it off
From Junior Brown to Dr Dre
And You Am I along the way
The music only made me want to get inside your touch
I'd rather go blind, I'd rather go blind
Than see you with another guy

You robbed me of my peace of mind
Stole the taste out of the wine
You left with nothing but you took it all
Now if you sleep with someone else
I just hope it's with another girl
You know I can't compete with that at all
I'd rather go blind, I'd rather go blind
Than see you with another guy

SHE ANSWERS THE SUN (LAZYBONES)

HIM Wake up lazybones
I've been watching you and wandering
And now the morning's gone
Hello lazybones
I've never known someone to sleep so long beneath the sun
Open your eyes now, I'm on your stairs
Look what I've brought you, mangoes and pears
Coffee and kisses for your freckles and red hair

HER Sticks and stones may hurt my bones
But names you know will never ever hurt me
Call me lazybones
I don't mind 'cause lazybones I was born to be
I need my beauty and beauty needs sleep
So go from my window my beauty to keep
Freckles and red hair, they're only skin deep

HIM Open your eyes now
HER I need my sleep
HIM Look what I've brought you
HER They're yours to keep
HIM Freckles and red hair
HER They're only skin deep

BEAT OF YOUR HEART

Here it comes again, the burning in the blood
The pounding in my brain, the rising of the flood
Every night I pray, begging sleep to come
But it's so far away
Way behind the drumbeat of your heart

I remember well a night of falling snow
Reading you a tale from Edgar Allen Poe
By the firelight, how your dark eyes shone
I had no idea it would be so strong
The beat of your heart!

Your midnight cry, your morning song
Your salty tears, your honey tongue
Every night I pray, begging sleep to come
But it's so far away
Way behind the drumbeat of your heart

GLORY BE TO GOD

Here comes the one that I adore—Glory be to God!
And I'm the one she's come here for—Glory be to God!
Throws her arms around my neck, oh Glory be to God!
Presses in against my chest—Glory be to God!
Glory be to God! Glory be to God!

She's got a smile that shames the sun—Glory be to God!
Undoes her buttons one by one—Glory be to God!
On my knees before her splendour, oh Glory be to God!
She knows she's a natural wonder—Glory be to God!
Glory be to God! Glory be to God!

Her eyes closed in trust above me—Glory be to God!
We both start shaking like a leaf on a tree, oh Glory be to God!
Glory be to God! Glory be to God! Glory be to God!

SATURDAY NIGHT AND SUNDAY MORNING

She's a screamer but no one knows
Just me and her old boyfriends I suppose
When I take her to see the folks they eat from her hand
On the way home I'm driving
I have to stop the car or crash it right there
She's my sticky treat, she's my bag o' sweets
She's my medicine
Oh she's Saturday night and Sunday morning

Like Princess Grace in Rear Window
She's a volcano under snow
Sometimes our action's all slo-mo in holy candlelight
I give her all my devotion
But sometimes she can't wait to be mashing on me
She's country soul, she's jelly roll
She's mountain high, she's valley low
Oh she's Saturday night and Sunday morning

She's heroin, she's amphetamine
She's mountain high, she's valley low
She's my sticky treat, she's my medicine
She's my medicine, she's my murder scene
She's Saturday night and Sunday morning

CHARLIE OWEN'S SLIDE GUITAR

I was crawling, in need of inspiration
So disgusted, aching for a cure
Right there in my neighbourhood
A spell from the old, dark wood
Charlie Owen's slide guitar

The usual murmurs, the clinking of the glasses
The usual rumours drifting round the bar
He made the same mistake twice
My tears took me by surprise
Charlie Owen's slide guitar

Charlie, I can't see your face
Your good friends are in disgrace
And at the crossroads I am told
The devil's waiting for your soul

If I ever find my way to heaven
I promise I'll throw a party there
The band will be from Brazil
I know he'll be sitting in as well
Charlie Owen with his slide guitar

MELTING
WRITTEN WITH MONIQUE BRUMBY

At the back of my grandmother's house there was a hill
With a tangled garden, thick and wild
We used to go there, you and I, as children
Slipping away from the aunts and uncles and their
   homemade brew
We carried our ice creams in the summer sun
Trying to make them last as long as we could
Pretty soon they started to run
Dripping down our arms, dripping on the ground
Melting

We sat under the trees smoking bark
Lighting little fires and stompin' each one out
As the summer went on the flames grew higher
We just stared and stared and stared at everything melting
Melting

At the back of my grandmother's house there was a hill
Black and smoking at the end of the day
We watched the fire trucks go back on down the road
We heard them calling out our names
We were standing in the shadows, melting
Melting, melting

Now my grandmother's house is a supermarket
And I'm far away, living in a colder city
And tonight I've pulled the top off a bottle of beer
And I've lit a fire and I'm staring, staring
Where are you, where are you now?
You're melting, we're all melting, melting, melting, melting

WOULD YOU BE MY FRIEND?

If I fell into confusion
Got scared but couldn't say
If I lost my rhyme and reason
And threw away the gift of grace
Would you be my friend?

If they said I don't deserve you
That my credit was no good
If they told you I'm not worthy of your love
And you should cut me like you cut dead wood
Would you be my friend?

And if you heard that I was on the town
Pissing loudly on your name
Would you find me, would you face me down?
Though your ears burned with shame
Would you be my friend?

And if I said I wished I'd never been born
And my mouth could only curse
If I'd passed the point of no return
Like a poor, puking child in church
Would you be my friend?
Right until the end
My only friend

YOU BROKE A BEAUTIFUL THING

Like a child acting so carelessly
You destroyed something you just didn't see
I'm not angry
How could I be angry with a child?

You broke a beautiful thing
And it won't ever mend

Thoughtless child
All wrapped up in the shape of a man
I tried so hard to get you to understand
I'm so sorry
Why am I always the one saying sorry
Like a mother does for a child?

You broke a beautiful thing
And it won't ever mend
I'll never have the pieces again

I hate the way I keep losing things
And I hate the way when I lose something
I never seem to find it again

You broke a beautiful thing

LAST NIGHT I LAY DREAMING

Last night I lay dreaming of you lying by my side
Your hair on my shoulder, our limbs all entwined
The gentle rising of your breast, the swell and dying fall
The night so deep and dark and pouring good on all
I wish that I could sleep and never wake again
For my love has gone forever far from pain

Last night I lay dreaming you were calling out your love
Telling me and all the world and God above
From the dream I woke up only holding on to air
The crying of the wind was all that I could hear
Oh that I could sleep and never wake again
And join my love who's gone from sorrow and from pain

Oh come, my love, tonight and rise up from the cold, cold clay
Dress your bones in flesh that never melts away
Softly creep into my bed and wake me with your breath
And together we will love and laugh at death
When the morning comes I know that you'll be gone
And when the moon is riding high you'll come again

HIGH WILD WAYS

WRITTEN WITH SPENCER P. JONES AND RENEE GEYER

Walking on grey sand
By the cold sea
Under a low sky
That's where you'll find me
Watching the sea birds play
Above the ocean spray
I love their high, wild ways

I wear your old shirt
Since we've been apart
And I keep a close watch
On this old heart
Counting down all the days
Until you come back again
I miss your high, wild ways

I close my eyes
And already I am flying
Like a wild bird on the wing
Straight to your arms
In the time it takes an eye to blink
All of a sudden losing everything
When I open them again

You said that you'll send back
A present for me
Some fine thing
From France or Italy
Oh hurry home, don't delay
No gift do I need these days
Only your high, wild ways

I WASTED TIME

I wasted time, now time is wasting me
One question left—to be or not to be
I cheated time and now it's time to pay
All out of change and less and less to say

I see old friends at funerals now and then
It's down to this—it's either me or them
I was a handsome raver in my time
Oh girl, you should have seen me in my prime

Yeah I wasted time
I thought it came for free
Now it's closing time
Won't you pray for me?

Molly took my hand and led the way
Now Molly's yellow hair is silver-grey
She wore a red dress she let me undo
But Molly swears that day her dress was blue

Yeah I wasted time
And time has wasted me
Now it's closing time
Won't you stay with me?

I tell you there's no failure like success
And there's no success like failure too I guess

WHISTLING BIRD

Never ever see you
Never see you no more

Never even knew you
Never knew you at all

I got a bird that whistles
I got a bird that sings

Rolling tires on the highway
Sounding like a choir

Fell asleep by the roadside
Woke up to a choir

LET ME IN

Let me in, I'm knocking at your door
Let me in, I'm knocking at your door

They told me you were shy and I said that's fine
I've never had a problem with the silent kind
But something tells me it could take a long, long time
For you to let me come inside

Let me in, I'm knocking at your door
Let me in, I'm knocking at your door

I spoke to a friend who said he'd speak to you
I was hoping that the message would get through
But you keep acting like you don't have a clue
I'm gonna have to use voodoo

Let me in, I'm knocking at your door
Let me in, I'm knocking at your door

Remember the walls down in Jericho
At last they fell to the ground
When you hear the humming, tell me where are you gonna go
I'm gonna tear your fortress down

Let me in, I'm knocking at your door
Let me in, I'm knocking at your door

BE CAREFUL WHAT YOU PRAY FOR

Be careful what you pray for
You just might get it
Be careful what you pray for
You might regret it
You get your hands on that glittering prize
Now everybody's coming at you from every side
Be careful what you pray for
You just might get it

Be careful what you want now
You might be sorry
Be careful what you want now
You might be sorry
You finally make it to your place in the sun
You stop and look around you—you're friends
    with no one
Be careful what you want now
You might be sorry

Go ahead like a moth to the flame
Go ahead

Be careful what you dream on
Dreams come true
Be careful what you dream on
They can turn on you
Revenge is a dish they say best tasted cold
But revenge digs two graves, makes a young person old
Be careful what you dream on
It might come true

IF I COULD START TODAY AGAIN

All the kings and queens in the bible
They could not turn back time
So what chance have I of a miracle
In this life of mine
I only want one day
To unsay the things I said
Undo the thing I did
Twenty-four little hours
Oh God! Please take them all away
And I promise I will change
If I could start today again

I know I'm not the milk and honey kind
Today I proved it true
When the red mist falls around my eyes
I know not what I do
Please give me back today
I won't say the things I said
Or do the thing I did
Every minute every hour
The replay's just the same
And I can't stand the shame
Oh let me start today again

I only want one day
One lousy day that's all
Of every day that's been before
Since time began
I know my prayer's in vain
But for a second I'll pretend
That I can start today again

INDEX OF TITLES

INDEX OF FIRST LINES